"Until what?"

"The truth comes out," he stated. "Besides, you need me."

"What makes you say that?" Now she really was interested in hearing his answer.

He loosened his grip enough to thump his thumb on the wheel. "You can't be certain you're out of danger."

"No one has tried anything so far," she pointed out.

"Because you've been with me," he said, like everyone should be on the same page.

She wasn't. Being with him caused her to want things she knew better than to want, and she'd only been around the man roughly twenty-four hours. Imagine how she would feel if she spent days or weeks alone with Dillen.

"That's a fair point, but it doesn't prove anything," she said.

"You have a shadow whether you like it or not," he insisted, clearly digging his heels in.

MURDER IN TEXAS

USA TODAY Bestselling Author

BARB HAN

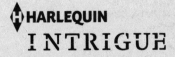

HARLEQUIN
INTRIGUE

All my love to Brandon, Jacob and Tori, who are the great loves
of my life. To Samantha for the bright shining light that you are.

To Babe, my hero, for being my best friend, greatest love and my
place to call home. I love you with everything that I am. Always
and forever.

To Shaq and Kobi, the best (and barkiest) writing buddies ever.

HARLEQUIN®
INTRIGUE™

Recycling programs
for this product may
not exist in your area.

ISBN-13: 978-1-335-59127-2

Murder in Texas

Copyright © 2023 by Barb Han

Harlequin Enterprises ULC
22 Adelaide St. West, 41st Floor
Toronto, Ontario M5H 4E3, Canada
www.Harlequin.com

Printed in U.S.A.

USA TODAY bestselling author **Barb Han** lives in north Texas with her very own hero-worthy husband, three beautiful children, a spunky golden retriever/standard poodle mix and too many books in her to-read pile. In her downtime, she plays video games and spends much of her time on or around a basketball court. She loves interacting with readers and is grateful for their support. You can reach her at barbhan.com.

Books by Barb Han

Harlequin Intrigue

The Cowboys of Cider Creek

Rescued by the Rancher
Riding Shotgun
Trapped in Texas
Texas Scandal
Trouble in Texas
Murder in Texas

A Ree and Quint Novel

Undercover Couple
Newlywed Assignment
Eyewitness Man and Wife
Mission Honeymoon

An O'Connor Family Mystery

Texas Kidnapping
Texas Target
Texas Law
Texas Baby Conspiracy
Texas Stalker
Texas Abduction

Visit the Author Profile page at Harlequin.com.

CAST OF CHARACTERS

Liz Hayes—Someone needs her erased...but who and why?

Dillen "Pitbull" Bullard—How far will he go to find out what truly happened to his father?

Mr. William Bullard—What actually happened to Mr. Bullard?

Keith Knolls—How vengeful is this spoiled rich ex-boyfriend?

Douglas Martin—Is he really a caring neighbor, or does he have a secret?

Margaret Coker—This older widow is acting strange... What does she know?

Chapter One

A December cold front arrived in Cider Creek at almost exactly the same moment as Liz Hayes. Mother Nature had decided to punctuate the sentence with sleet. Liz turned down her music so she could see better. Clouds covered the sun, making it dark outside for four o'clock in the afternoon. Pea-size hail pelted her windshield as the temperature gauge on the dashboard dropped before her eyes while she sat at the first red light past town.

Liz tightened her grip on the steering wheel. Being in her hometown was hard enough without the weather reminding her that she should have stayed home instead of taking this trip. Houston wasn't far, but she rarely came back to her old stomping grounds to visit. Her jerk of a grandfather was to blame, but she didn't want to think about him right now as she impatiently tapped her thumb on the wheel.

Traffic lights in small towns could last forever. This one felt like it had been red for an eternity. Under normal circumstances, she would appreciate being as delayed as possible. Driving in bad weather had her nerves on edge. The conditions were getting worse by the minute. In fact, she rolled her window down to get a feel for how cold it had become.

A sudden glow from the construction site to her left caught her attention. The lights must have been automatic, turning on now that it was almost pitch black. There was a noise coming from the area, too. She strained to listen. It wasn't a noise so much as what sounded like a call for help—one that got louder and more desperate sounding the second time she heard it.

Liz tapped the button to turn on her hazard lights before pulling to the side of the road, opening her door and exiting her five-year-old Honda Accord. As she bolted toward what sounded like a male voice, a rogue thought that this could be some kind of setup struck. Setup for what, though? Crime in this small town was almost nonexistent. Her mind was probably playing tricks on her.

Either way, someone was in trouble.

As she neared the voice, she heard the fragility. A twinge of recognition dawned. This person was familiar even though she couldn't quite place him as rain came down like needles against her skin. Wind gusted. She put up an arm to block against flying debris in case it came at her, too.

"Hello?" she shouted against the storm.

Liz reached the open lot. A structure that looked a lot like a small strip mall was in the early stages of development. Strange how she expected everything to stay the same since the last time she'd been here. Towns, like life, moved on.

Scanning the area, she didn't see anyone. No one responded to her, either. She called out again and then listened. A half dozen thoughts fought for center stage in her mind. Was the person unconscious? Were they gone? Was the cry for help an echo that had traveled across the mostly bare lot? She didn't want to question whether or not the person was dead. Were they? Alive yet buried?

A knot twisted in her stomach so tight she could scarcely breathe. Adrenaline coursed through her, causing her hands to shake. Liz reminded herself not to let her imagination run wild.

"Is anyone out here?" she asked. Sheetrock was stacked several feet high in spots near the metal beams that were beginning to look like what the structure would end up being. The person could be lying behind one of those.

There was a hunter-green porta potty in the middle of what looked to be a future parking lot. Wood was staked into the ground, marking something. Liz had no idea what. And there were piles of rocks, big and small, pretty much everywhere.

Maybe she was hearing things, losing her mind. The stress of having her small accessory company's sales take off in the past year was clearly doing her in. Sales had gone through the roof, and she felt like she was paddling against a hurricane to keep up. She'd been handling the business well. Or so she believed. Orders were going out on time. The major retailer who'd picked up her line of *Just Totin'* bags seemed happy so far. She'd had to ramp up production on what had felt like a moment's notice.

Liz and her controlling grandfather might have been opposites in almost every way, but she credited him with passing down incredible business sense. She was building her company from the ground up with no outside help, much in the same way he'd done for his successful cattle-ranching business. Duncan Hayes might have been a jerk, but he'd been shrewd. A twinge of guilt struck at calling him a jerk now that he was gone.

Liz sighed. She assumed the family meeting she'd been called home to take had to do with figuring out what to do with the cattle ranch and inheritances—money she didn't want or need because she hadn't earned it. Her mile-long stubborn streak had probably come from her grandfather as well.

Gravel crunched underneath her boots as she circled the construction site. This wasn't the time to regret wearing heels. At least her feet were dry and warm as another gust of wind snapped around her, whipping hair so dark it almost faded into the night around her. Strands stuck in her eyelashes as Mother Nature's wrath sent larger chunks of hail crashing into Liz.

Turning toward the sedan she'd abandoned, she decided to retreat while she still had a hint of pride left and before her vehicle ended up on the back of a tow truck.

"He-e-e-lp me." The weak voice came from behind her. Liz whirled around to a spot she'd missed when she'd been circling the area. A cold shiver raced through her as she bolted toward the sound.

As she rounded a stack of sheet metal that was backed up to a pile of gravel, a bolt of lightning cut sideways across the sky. There it was, plain as day…a human hand sticking out of the gravel. Was he stuck underneath heavy Sheetrock? Wedged in somehow?

Another wind gust caused wood to come flying from seemingly out of nowhere. Visibility in this area was next to nothing since there was no light in this part of the construction zone. The last thing she wanted to do was step on the hand. She instinctively checked her pockets for her phone, then remembered it was still inside her car.

"I'm here," she said, hearing the panic in her own voice. "Hold on. Okay?" *Please don't die.*

Staying rooted to her spot, she bent down and searched for the hand where she'd last seen it. The second she found it, fingers closed around her. A moment of pure panic struck at the thought she might not be in time to save this person. Pushing through her anxiety, she offered reassurances as she started digging him out.

A pair of headlights illuminated her vehicle on the road. She shouted and waved, but the truck went around her car and kept going. No one wanted to be out in this mess for longer than they had to.

Resolve replaced fear as she let go of the hand so she could use both of hers to move the gravel. A person was wedged underneath the Sheetrock.

"Hold on, okay?" Liz asked, but it was more state-ment than question. "I'm going to get you out of here."

In the dark, it was impossible to get a good look at the man's face. Based on the feel of the skin on his hands, he wasn't young. Not old, either. Middle aged? His hand was like ice. She was already shiv-ering from the cold. At least the hail had let up. Bad storms in Texas had a way of blowing right through faster than a roller coaster at Six Flags.

The reprieve from being hit in the face every few seconds was welcomed.

The man mumbled something unintelligible.

The likelihood she was going to get him out at her slow rate of progress was slim.

What else could she find to dig him out? There had to be something around here to work with. This was, after all, a construction site. Wouldn't there be tools? She scanned over by the well-lit areas. Saw nothing.

Since she was in a praying mood, she went ahead and sent up a request for an ambulance and maybe a forklift operator. Trying to lift the heavy construc-tion materials off the man by hand would be impos-sible. The most she could do was make it budge the tiniest bit.

There was no choice but to run back to her car and call for help, no matter how much she hated leaving him here alone. Would he understand her if she told him the new plan?

"I have to call for help. I'll be right back," she said, finding the hand again. There wasn't much life to it, but a small squeeze of reassurance gave her hope that he was still fighting. "Hold tight."

Liz stood up and then turned around, ready to make the run back to her sedan. Lightning flashed. She gasped as she stared at the chest of a man.

"Oh, hell no," he said as she fisted her hands at her sides, ready to fight back.

Another voice came up behind her. She felt a blow to the side of her head. And then everything went dark.

DILLEN "PIT BULL" BULLARD paid the cab driver, exited the vehicle and then shouldered his rucksack. On a sharp sigh, he tucked his chin to his chest and headed toward the double glass doors at Cider Creek General Hospital.

Five days had passed since his father's accident. It had taken two days to get word to him where he'd been deployed and three to get back home. *Home?* He almost laughed out loud. Cider Creek, Texas, was the furthest thing from being his real home. He'd grown up here. Hated every minute of a childhood where he hadn't fit in. And couldn't get out fast enough.

There was no reason to feel sorry for himself. He'd found his calling with the United States military as an army ranger. *Rangers Lead the Way.* Considering his father had been fighting for his life for five days with Dillen almost as far away as a person could be, he couldn't help but think he'd failed.

Dillen was here now. He'd convinced his supervising officer to let him skip the normally requisite visit to the alpaca farm in east Texas where he could cool off so he wouldn't reach for a weapon on instinct if someone tapped him on the shoulder in a grocery store line. Coming in hot meant he'd have to manage his emotions. Living in a hot zone for months on end had a way of making a solider prepared for any kind of fight, even when diplomacy was the best course of action.

A receptionist sat behind a bar-height circular counter. A twelve-foot Christmas tree twinkled to his left. Signs of yesterday's holiday were everywhere. To say he wasn't in the yuletide spirit was the understatement of the year.

The attendant's back was to him, and she was playing a game on her cell. He'd been to this place many times in as a kid, always as a patient and mostly because of fighting. Going into the military had given him a positive outlet for his anger. Ranger school had exhausted him and taught him how to channel his rage at something productive—a real enemy and not some kid who'd made a smart remark about how poor Dillen and his father had been. Or how his dad couldn't keep a woman around. Jerks. The grown-up version of him realized that now.

He cleared his throat to get the lady's attention. She swatted like there was a fly buzzing beside her.

"I'll be with you in a minute," she said, clearly irritated by the interruption.

Did she just disrespect him?

A coil tightened in Dillen's chest. He smacked his flat palm down onto the counter. The receptionist jumped. She spun around in her chair, phone still in hand. The *go straight to hell* look he shot her got attention. It probably didn't hurt that he was still wearing full operational camouflage. Her eyes widened as she got a good look at him.

"May I help you?" she asked, her voice cracking enough for him to realize she was afraid.

He didn't know how to turn down the level of intensity, so he stood there practically glaring at her. "My father is here. William Bullard. I'm told he isn't doing well."

"Oh, right," she said, like that explained his intense mood. People not doing their jobs while they were on the clock sent white-hot anger roaring through him.

Dillen took in a couple of deep breaths while he watched her roll up to the computer and tap keys on the keyboard.

"The waiting room is on the fifth floor," she said without looking up at him. "You can't miss it." She pointed toward an elevator bank. "Those will take you where you want to go. Just don't forget he's on five, and you'll be fine."

"Thank you, ma'am," he said. His Southern manners were ingrained in him now. *Ma'am* and *sir* were instilled in his vocabulary from his time in the military. He would have thought growing up in a small Texas town would have done the trick. It hadn't hurt. He'd been rebellious enough to fight using any sign of respect.

Dillen walked over to the elevators and then pushed the button to go up. At ten o'clock at night, it didn't take long. The hallways on the ground floor were almost empty, too. The *ding* sounded, and doors opened. Dillen walking inside and pushed the number 5. The ride was short. He could use a cup of coffee. But first he needed to see his father. Too many years had gone by without Dillen keeping in touch in the way he should have. In the way a good son would have.

So many *could haves* and *should haves*.

Dillen bit back a curse, clenching his teeth to keep from saying something he shouldn't and adding to the list of regrets.

The last thing he remembered about being home was how much he couldn't stand the Hayes family and their holier-than-thou attitude. They were everything he wasn't. The boys had been athletes and made good grades in school. The girls had been picture perfect and way out of his league. Then again, he hadn't had a league back in high school. He'd had raging hormones compounded by the fact he'd lived in a town where he never belonged. His father hadn't belonged. Dillen had been picked on, made fun of and generally tortured until he'd filled out his six-feet-three-inch frame. Then, he'd signed up for the military before he could take out his revenge on the jerks who'd made his life miserable and wind up in jail.

There was one Hayes in particular he couldn't stand more than the others. Liz Hayes had been in his grade and was everything he despised about the small town. She was privilege times ten and knew it. All she'd had to do was bat an eyelash for one of the jocks to rush over to pick up her pencil if it had dropped on the floor. It had been disgusting the way his classmates had been ready to jump if she'd snapped her fingers.

The elevator dinged, jolting him back to reality and out of his quick trip down memory lane. He realized his hands were fisted, and he clenched his back teeth so hard he thought they might crack if he didn't ease up.

So, yeah, he was ready for battle.

Dillen forced a couple of slow breaths as the doors opened. There was a nurses' station immediately in front of him. He assumed the waiting room would be off to the side. Maybe he could swing by his father's room rather than sit in a blue-and-white room with burnt coffee sitting on warmers.

There were two nurses at their station. As soon as he stepped out of the elevator bank, they studied him as though a warning call had been made from downstairs.

"The waiting room is right over there," one of the nurses said. "We've alerted Dr. Lawrence that you've arrived. He's on his way."

Dillen nodded and thanked them. It might've been best to be briefed by the doctor before he saw his father in person. Although part of him wanted to explain to the nurses there wasn't much that could shock him considering what he did for a living.

He stopped halfway across the hallway and turned. "Coffee?"

"There should be some already brewed in there,"

the nurse said. The somber tone had him concerned. "If not, let me know and I'll put on a pot."

After thanking them again, he walked into the sterile, white-tiled room with blue chairs. The room was empty save for one woman with a large bandage on her head. She looked up, and his hands fisted.

What the hell was Liz Hayes doing here?

Chapter Two

Liz stood up the minute Dillen Bullard walked into the room, surprised at how quickly her pulse climbed. The man was over six feet tall and built with stacked muscles on top of lean hips. His dark hair was cut tight, and he had the most piercing pair of hazel eyes—eyes that were surprisingly soft on a face of hard angles and planes. Military fatigues made the green hue in his eyes pop. He was all broad chest, solid arms and slim waist. If it wasn't Dillen Bullard standing there, she might've thought he was the sexiest man she'd seen in a long time. Maybe ever.

Chalking up her physical reaction to a stress response at seeing the person who'd mercilessly picked on her growing up, Liz mentally shook it off. Besides, she hadn't backed down then and she wouldn't now as he stood there with his arms crossed, studying her.

"I'd ask what you're doing here, but the bandage on your head tells me you're a patient," he said before heading toward the coffee machine.

For a split second, she debated whether or not to

tell him the real reason she'd been in this waiting room for five days straight without a shower and skipped Christmas with her family yesterday. A few spritzes of perfume had kept her from stinking up the place.

Dillen poured a cup of fresh brew and stood rooted to his spot as he took the first sip. She couldn't help but notice he kept one eye on her the whole time.

"True," she finally said, folding her arms and hugging them to her chest. "How do you explain the fact I was treated and released five days ago yet am still here, waiting for Mr. Bullard to wake up?"

The look he shot her could have frozen water on the sidewalk during a Texas summer. She shook it off.

"I was there at the construction site," she said before Dr. Lawrence walked in the room, stopping all conversation. Since she wasn't next of kin, the doctor couldn't tell her anything about Mr. Bullard's condition even though she'd slipped in his room a couple of times when the night nurse was busy.

A look of shock flashed across Dillen's features before he refocused on the man in scrubs. Dillen's jaw muscle clenched like he was biting back something he wanted to say. At his height and with the way he took up space in a room, most people would be intimidated. Not Liz. So, she dropped her arms to her sides and turned toward the doctor.

The look on Dr. Lawrence's face as he made a beeline for Dillen with an outstretched hand caused her stomach lining to braid. Introductions were made after a handshake. The doctor was middle aged and half a foot shorter than Dillen. He was slim and serious with small specs for glasses. Dillen seemed to sense the news wasn't going to be good. His face was stone-cold sober as he asked how his father was doing.

"Mr. Bullard sustained multiple contusions to his frontal—"

"Can you give it to me in plain English, please, sir?" Dillen asked. His deep, even timbre washed over her. It wasn't something she could risk paying too much attention to or she might actually stop resenting the guy. This seemed like a good time to remind herself that she was here for a lonely old man whose son was deployed. Plus, she respected Dillen for his service. It was impossible to hate him. He appeared to have cleaned up his life even though his attitude toward her hadn't changed, which was exactly the reason she had every intention of keeping him at arm's length.

Dr. Lawrence looked Dillen straight in the eyes. He shook his head. "I'm sorry to inform you that your father passed away twenty minutes ago." He paused for a beat. "We did everything possible to save him."

All the muscles in Dillen's body tensed. He took in a breath that looked like it was meant to calm a rage building inside him, as though guilt threatened to eat him from the inside out. "I was briefed as to how he ended up in the hospital, but I have questions."

"According to the file, this young lady found him on a construction site covered in rubble during a sleet storm," the doctor said. "Flying debris may have been responsible."

Dillen nodded and his jaw muscle clenched. "I appreciate everything you did for my father."

"I couldn't be sorrier," Dr. Lawrence said as tears welled in Liz's eyes. "Would you like to speak to someone in the clergy?"

"No. Thank you, sir," Dillen said, his voice even like he'd switched to autopilot. Her chest squeezed and her heart ached.

The doctor excused himself after saying someone would be coming to take Dillen to his father in a few minutes.

Dillen swallowed the rest of the contents of his cup and then crushed the foam in his hand before chunking it into the trash. He dropped his backpack onto a chair and then walked over to the window, raking his hands through his hair.

There were so many things Liz wanted to say, but her mouth couldn't form the words. *I'm sorry* seemed hollow and lacking. Before she could think, he whirled around on her.

"What were you doing at the construction site?" he asked, his tone accusing. Those hazel eyes appraised her, causing heat to flood her.

Considering the fact he'd just been told his father was gone, she didn't feel the need to split hairs about his tone of voice.

"That's a good question," she responded. "The sheriff believes this was an accident."

"You don't?" he asked, studying her.

"I left my car on the side of the road at a red light in a sleet storm after hearing a call for help," she said. "Apparently, someone called 911 but didn't stop because the storm was getting worse. That's as much as I know since I must have also been hit with debris. I can't remember much else about that afternoon other than the fact I was on my way back to my family's ranch."

"But you don't believe it's as simple as that," he said.

"No. I don't," she admitted. "It's strange. Don't you think?"

He shrugged. "I have no idea. I landed an hour ago and made my way here. I was told there was an accident, and that's about all I know."

"I have questions," she said.

"Meaning?" he asked. His posture said he was still a bundle of tension and coiled so tightly that it wouldn't take much for him to snap. She couldn't blame him for his frustration and sadness. He'd traveled a long way to receive devastating news.

"What was I doing at a construction site in the first place?" she asked. "Not to mention the fact I'm still confused as to what your father would have been doing there when a storm was on its way." She shrugged. "He's not connected to the job in any way. So, why go?"

"What did the sheriff say?" he asked. "I'm assuming you mentioned your concerns."

She blew out a breath.

"I'm not sure why he believes what he does," she said honestly. "I guess it wraps the situation up in a nice bow." She paused for a beat. "It just doesn't scan right for me." She tried to ignore the headache trying to form in between her eyes. Blinking a couple of times didn't help. Neither did the overhead fluorescent lighting in the room.

Her eyes burned. "I'm not trying to cause trouble here. None of the explanations make sense. I mean, I'm supposed to have abandoned my vehicle based on realizing someone needed help, but there must have been thunder and lightning. So how did I hear your father? And then why wouldn't I be the one to call 911 if I had concerns? According to the sheriff, a concerned citizen saw my vehicle and called for help. That much, I can believe based on the weather reports. Your father was supposed to have been buried in debris and I was also hit. But I have bruises that don't match up with what was supposed to have happened to me. Then there's my head injury. Wouldn't I duck if debris was flying at me?"

"Why would you even care about my dad?" he asked with the venom of a snake bite.

She bit back the urge to call him out on his preconceived notion of her. Once again, she reminded herself that he'd lost someone he loved. She knew what it was like to lose a parent, except that she'd been too young to remember much about her father.

"Because when I asked the hospital staff how your father was doing, they shook their heads. I came into the waiting room to offer sympathy, and no one was here," she said with a little more ire than intended. She couldn't help it. Dillen got under her skin more than she wanted to admit. "No one should be alone over the holidays."

THOSE WORDS WERE the equivalent of knife stabs to the center of Dillen's chest. He stood even straighter and clenched his fists. "I was on my way as soon as I received word."

"And here you are," she said with a curt tone. He was being dismissed by the raven-haired woman—a woman who'd grown up from a spindly-legged child with long hair and dark-roast eyes. She had on jeans that covered long legs and a sweater that hugged full breasts. Under normal circumstances, she was exactly the kind of person he would want to get to know better. But this was Liz Hayes, and her attitude toward him was a bucket of ice water. After all these years, she still looked down her nose at him.

"Then you can go," he said before it clicked that she might've been the only witness to what had happened to his father—a father who was gone now. Those last words were more physical blows.

Dillen issued a sharp sigh as she stood there, tapping her toe.

"But I hope you won't," he said as a nurse entered the room.

"Mr. Bullard," she began reverently, "I can take

you to see your father now." Her tone matched the occasion and was a stark reminder of his loss.

Dillen nodded even though he couldn't seem to get his feet to move. He caught Liz's gaze and held on to it. Would she be here when he returned? He didn't have the right to ask her, so he turned and walked out of the room behind the nurse.

It dawned on him that Liz had stuck around when his father had needed someone and Dillen had just treated her like she'd been the one to hurt his dad. Jerk move on Dillen's part. Part of him hoped she would stick around so he could apologize. Based on the bandage on her forehead, she'd been through hell and back. She said she didn't remember exactly what happened. Although that could change. He wasn't an expert at head injuries, but he'd experienced or witnessed his fair share. One of his buddies had forgotten how to speak for a week after being knocked in the head with a piece of metal. His speech had come back as though nothing had ever happened.

Time slowed on the walk down the long hallway. Dillen's mind snapped back to the past, to all those Sunday pizza dinners. They'd always had pizza on Sundays. Every night had had a meal assigned to it. Routine had been the staple of his father's existence. There hadn't been much in the way of money, but there'd been food on the table every night. The government had provided Dillen's breakfast and lunches while at school. It was most likely part of the reason he'd signed up for the military after high school graduation instead of working in town or on a ranch.

He'd figured he owed some loyalty, that the government deserved to be paid back for their investment.

Routine had also the bane of Dillen's childhood.

During high school, he'd tried to talk his father into driving two towns over to grocery shop at one of those big box stores. He'd tried to convince his old man that the cheap prices had made up for the extra gas. But Pop had waved him off, saying Tuesdays were for the grocery store in Cider Creek. Dillen had been embarrassed for his friends to see they'd been on government assistance.

His part-time job cleaning out stalls had earned him the nickname Bullcrap from the jocks at school. It had been replaced by Pit Bull once he'd joined the service for his ability to lock onto a target with relentless force. All the bullying in school had given him the drive to push his body to its limits and become the strongest human he could possibly be.

It also had also him enough anger to last a lifetime. He'd taken some of it out on Liz in the waiting room. Dillen owed her an apology.

The nurse stopped in front of room 501.

"Take all the time you need," she said. "Hit the call button when you're ready." She didn't explain further as she spoke softly. The rest was obvious. His father's body would be taken to the morgue. "Someone from administration will be waiting at the nurse's station for your instructions on how you would like to handle the details."

He thanked her before stepping inside the room. An emptiness filled his chest like when he'd been five years old and had watched his mother walk out and into the cab of a waiting U-Haul. The memory gutted him, even after all these years.

Dillen walked to his father's bedside, sat down and then reached for his hand. Closing his eyes, he could imagine them sitting at the table, talking about all those stupid little things people talked about like gas prices and the weather. Funny how people never discussed anything important or noticed how much they would miss someone until they were gone.

A few tears spilled down Dillen's cheeks as he bent forward and rested his head on their joined hands. He would give ten years off the back end of his life to be able to tell his father the words neither had uttered out loud in his thirty-two years of life. He would tell his father that he loved him.

Minutes passed before Dillen could pull himself together enough to sit up straight again.

"Hey, Pop," he began. It didn't matter that his father couldn't hear. "Remember that time I hid in the closet in your room and ended up trapping myself inside?" He paused for a few beats, remembering all the times he'd been a jerk to his father. The teenage years had been the worst. His temper had raged, and he'd hated everything about their life.

Dillen took in a couple of slow breaths so he could get the next part out without losing it.

"I wasn't scared, even though I didn't like being in tight places back then," he continued, a few rogue tears rolling down his cheeks, dripping onto the blanket one by one.

He squeezed his father's lifeless hand.

"Because I knew that you would come looking for me," he managed to get out as emotion knotted in his throat, making it hard to speak. "I wasn't afraid because I knew you would turn over the whole house until you found me, and I'd be okay."

Guilt and regret slammed into him at all the years he'd missed with his father. It had been too easy to leave Cider Creek and not look back. Keeping himself distracted and busy had made it too easy to lose track of what was really important. It had been too easy to turn his back on the one who'd stuck it out, unlike his other parent.

And now it was too late to get any of the missed time back. Too late to be the son his father had deserved to have. Too late to make it right between them.

His father wasn't supposed to be gone this soon.

Dillen sat there in silence for a long while, no longer counting the minutes as they passed.

Eventually, he stood up and let go of his father's hand. Then he said the words he should have a long time ago: "I love you, Pop."

It occurred to Dillen that he'd been inside the room for an hour. There was no way Liz would still be waiting around after all this time had passed. He didn't blame her, either. There had to be some way to look her up or ask for her number. As he walked down the hallway toward the nurse's station, her words cycled through his thoughts and his anger returned. Because she'd made it seem like there had been foul play involved. And he intended to find out why.

Being a notoriously private person, Hayes would make tracking her down a challenge. Many people lived their lives on social media by "checking in" to every restaurant, park and jogging trail. Not so for the Hayes family—not that he'd stalked them. It was common knowledge.

A man who resembled his father's neighbor stood at the elevators. Mr. Martin must've been getting ready for the cold because his gloves were already on. Dillen shoved the thought aside as the guy stepped into the elevator and then the doors closed behind him.

By chance, he peeked inside the waiting room just in case Liz was still there. As he'd expected, she was gone.

Chapter Three

Liz washed up in the fifth floor bathroom as best as she could and brushed her teeth. The lack of a real shower in more days than she cared to count made her want to soak in a hot bath for an entire evening. She'd slept in fits and starts. A real bed sounded like heaven.

After drying her hands and face, she applied ChapStick to dry lips. She figured Dillen might be in his father's room for a while longer, and she planned to stick around until they could have a conversation about the things that didn't add up. Then she could go home and face the family meeting with a clear conscience. As far as she remembered, Mr. Bullard had been a kind person. He'd never bothered anyone or asked for much. His job as a lab tech assistant couldn't have brought in a lot of money, but he'd managed to make ends meet and bring up a son on his own. He'd been an admirable person by anyone's standard.

The second she opened the door to the hallway, Dillen's masculine voice hit her full force. The deep baritone was smooth as whiskey over ice. She mentally shook off her physical reaction to him.

He stood with his back to her, speaking to one of the administrators. There was no hint of sadness in his tone despite the fact that he had to be torn apart by his father's death. Dillen hadn't made it in time to say goodbye, either. Those were the details that would haunt a man like Dillen for a long time to come.

His earlier anger subsided, most likely buried deep inside while he worked out the arrangements for his father.

The hospital administrator typed on the keyboard as he spoke. He must have heard the door open and close because he gave a sideways glance, performed a double take and then held a finger up to the staff member, indicating he'd be right back.

Dillen turned around. With the full force of those intense hazel eyes on her, Liz had to swallow to ease some of the sudden dryness in her throat.

"You didn't leave," he said with a hint of gratitude, which was another surprise coming from him. He'd been prickly to her a little while ago. It had caused her defenses to respond in kind and they'd had a tense exchange, but that wasn't going to stop her from doing the right thing.

"Bathroom," she managed to say in more of a croak than anything else.

"Will you stick around for a few minutes?" he asked. "I'd like to talk."

"That's why I'm here," she said, croak-free this time.

He nodded and then turned his attention back to the staff member, finishing up their conversation. Him turning his attention away from her was a lot like stepping into a cold, dark cave after being warmed by the sun.

There weren't any chairs in the hallway, so Liz made her way back into the waiting area. Bone weary, she was exhausted down to her toes. In fact, they ached along with the rest of her. The tiredness that she'd been keeping at bay was finally settling in now that Dillen had arrived. It was almost as if her body had gotten the message that she didn't have to push to stay awake any longer. Relief was here in the form of an army ranger.

At one point, a nurse had brought her a pillow and blanket. She retrieved them before curling up in the uncomfortable blue chair and rested her eyes. Before she knew it, she was out.

"Hey," Dillen said. His quiet but masculine voice roused her from sleep. She tried to sit up, but it was like moving in slow motion. Almost like her soul had left her body and she was left in some kind of strange haze. This wouldn't be a good time to ask her to balance the books of her business or stand on her two legs for that matter.

"Everything okay?" she managed to ask as she shook off some of the fog. Her eyelids were the equivalent of sandpaper. How long had she been out? Couldn't have been more than a couple of minutes.

"You need sleep," Dillen said with a hint of frustration in his voice. Excuse her for not being ready to talk after sitting in this room for the past five days. "Are you all right with me helping you to my vehicle?" He muttered a curse. "I just realized that I don't have anything to drive here."

"My Honda is outside," she said, wondering where this was going but too tired to put up much of a fight. "One of my brothers brought it to the hospital."

Dillen glanced around like he expected one of them to be standing around in the background.

"I wouldn't let them stay," she said. "And I don't want to go home this late." She wasn't as ready to face the Hayes family home as she'd believed.

"Would you be fine with me driving?" he asked.

She didn't think she had a problem with it. "To where?"

"A place where you can sleep on a comfortable bed," he said before adding, "and don't worry, I wouldn't try anything with someone like you."

Those last words were the equivalent of half a dozen bee stings on her face. She could ask him what the hell he meant later. Right now, a bed was too tempting to pass up, and she did need to have a serious conversation with the man. It would be easier to do if they were under the same roof.

"Good," she said. "Because I wouldn't let you get away with it anyway. And I can take the couch."

He mumbled something she couldn't quite hear.

"I'm going to help you up now," he said as she struggled to stand up. Dozing off had been a bad idea but she'd be fine in a few minutes. She glanced around. "My purse is over…" Well, hell, she couldn't remember where she'd last put it.

"It's underneath the chair. Do you want me to get it?" he asked.

She shook her head before bending down, with his help, and retrieving her handbag from underneath the chair. She shouldered the strap.

"Thank you," she said before pointing out the keys to her vehicle were inside.

"I have no intention of putting my hand where it doesn't belong," he argued. There was something to his tone that said he'd gotten himself into trouble with that one before. A woman's purse could definitely qualify as sacred ground. However, she'd expressly given him permission, which was a whole different story.

If she'd had the energy, she would have cracked a smile. Instead, she dug inside her handbag for the key fob so she could unlock the doors when they reached the lot. "Got it."

Now he picked her up with almost no effort on his part. The man's arms were like bands of steel, which wasn't something she wanted to focus on as he lifted her off her chair like he was the angry green version of Bruce Banner.

Dillen carried her to the Honda and then managed to place her inside the passenger seat without so much as bumping any of her body parts on the material surrounding the door, which made the huge bruise on her hip happy. Being pressed up against a solid wall of muscled chest caused her pulse to rise, though. She felt his heartbeat against her body, the pace matching her own.

"Go ahead and sleep on the way home if you want to," he said.

She nodded and closed her eyes after he helped her buckle up, not that she needed his or anyone else's permission to rest. When she got settled, she would need to let her family know she'd left the hospital so they didn't bring food or drop by as they had been. She'd had the chance to meet her new sisters-in-law. Even her baby sister had found an amazing person to share her life with, and Reese had been voted least likely to settle down first. Marriage and kids were good for some people. Liz had a business to run—one she'd been accused of choosing over her last serious boyfriend.

Since her mind decided to wander, she sat up a little straighter. Dillen claimed the driver's seat. She wasn't alert enough to trust herself behind the wheel, so it was good that he was the one doing the driving.

"Where are you taking me again?" she asked.

"To my father's house," he said. "I have no idea what condition it's in since I haven't been home in two years."

"Really?" she asked before she could reel the word back in.

"Why would you have a problem with that?" he asked as his face twisted with disdain. "I apologize if my family isn't as good as yours."

Liz wasn't touching that statement with a ten-foot pole.

DILLEN GRIPPED THE steering wheel until his knuckles went white. After his last statement—accusation, if he was being honest—Liz became quiet. Too quiet. It was the seething quiet that told him that he'd crossed a line that shouldn't have been touched.

Rather than address it, he figured he could do better by keeping his own mouth zipped. Besides, his anger shouldn't have been pointed at her since it hadn't been her fault to begin with.

"I'm a jerk for not getting here sooner," he finally said after a long pause. "An absolute waste as a son." His strained relationship with his father would haunt him for the rest of his life. Death was final, and there was no way to make it right now, to tell his father how much he appreciated him for sticking around when, apparently, parenting was optional once a kid was born. "That last comment I made was me taking out my frustration on you, and that's not okay." He wasn't quite ready to absolve her from having her nose into the air for her whole life, but she'd done what he hadn't—made certain his father hadn't been alone on his deathbed.

"I slipped into his room every night," she said. "Since I wasn't next of kin and he was in intensive care, I had to sneak."

"On my count, you spent the holiday in a waiting room for a man who wasn't even your father," he said, realizing he needed to rethink his position on her being a spoiled brat. Time would tell, but he was a big believer in watching people's actions instead of listening to their words.

"Yes," she admitted. "Is that a problem for you?"

Fair point, he decided. He'd probably had that one coming—and possibly more considering he'd shoved her into a category that he was thinking maybe she didn't belong in any longer.

"It means a lot that you would do something like that for someone who was a stranger," he said. "More to the point, that person was my father."

"Your dad wasn't a stranger to me," she said with confusion. "I knew him growing up."

"Why? How?" he asked.

"He worked at the lab, and I had to drop things off there sometimes for the cattle ranch," she said. "Your dad always greeted me with a warm smile and a wave. He was one of the nicest people." She paused after her voice cracked on those last few words. Next, she cleared her throat and sat up a little straighter. "He was just a good person and was always kind to me when I saw him around town."

Dillen didn't know what to say to that. Was there more to Liz than met the eye?

Before he went too far down the rabbit hole of caring, he pulled into the parking lot of the trailer park where he'd grown up. It wasn't a fancy ranch like the Hayes home. This was Cider Creek Park, but there wasn't anything park-like about the area. In fact, it was more gravel than anything else, which crunched underneath the car's tires at the moment.

"Not exactly the palace where you grew up," he quipped. "Think you can manage sticking around for a night here?"

Liz took in a slow breath.

"We should stick to the real reason we're being forced together instead of these backhanded insults you've been lobbing," she said with finality.

Had Dillen just been put in his place? He was partially amused.

"Sounds like a plan to me, princess," he quipped.

"Good. Then learn your place. And don't call me princess," she shot back. He'd riled her up. Good. She shouldn't get too comfortable around him because he'd just end up disappointing her much in the same way he'd done with his father.

An ache formed in his chest the size of the Grand Canyon and with the force of a hurricane as it sucked water out to sea. The water never came back in the same way it had left. It battered. It bruised. It flooded.

And that was exactly what Dillen would be to Liz. He would be trouble times ten. He would destroy her heart and her trust in all men. He would be the disappointment he'd always been to his own father.

Dillen parked next to the trailer he'd grown up in. This had been his childhood. It hadn't been filled with ponies and fancy birthday parties. It hadn't been filled with more friends than he'd known what to do with. It hadn't been filled with the kind of love Liz had surely experienced growing up a Hayes. It was a piece of…

He decided it was best not to say the word that would come next. It was probably better for everyone involved if he stuffed those thoughts down deep instead. This was the time he would normally hit the gym and get in a good workout to burn off much of his frustration. Talking had never been his thing. Lifting, pushing his body to the limit was the only time he got tired enough to relax, let alone sleep.

The trailer looked the same on the outside. It was white with neon-green trim like the relic from the eighties it was. Embarrassment flooded him. Why had he brought Liz Hayes here?

"This was a mistake," he said, reversing course. "You would probably be more comfortable in a hotel. There's one not too far from here off the highway."

"Why?" she asked as he put the gearshift in Park. "You think I'm too good to sleep in a trailer?" She issued a disgusted grunt. "Watch me."

Liz opened the car door and exited the Honda while the engine was still running. He cut it off, hopped out of the vehicle and hit the key fob to lock the doors.

"Look, you don't have to prove a point to me," he started. "I'm sure that you're fully capable of suffering a night or two inside a trailer just to prove you're one of the 'little' people."

She whirled around on him and poked a finger in his chest.

"Look here," she said. "I'm getting a little tired of this self-pity routine you have going. The one where you're a victim because you didn't grow up with money. Guess what? It's not the treat you think it is to be a Hayes. So, congratulations. You're just like everyone else in town who believes we're all entitled brats. Good for you. You figured us out. Do you want a prize now?"

He stood there for a long second dumbfounded.

Dillen knew exactly what he wanted. It wasn't a prize. It was a kiss. The way her gaze lingered on his lips while she slicked her tongue across hers said she did, too. So that was exactly what he did. He leaned in and pressed his lips to hers, waiting for the slap that might come next.

Chapter Four

Liz grabbed fistfuls of Dillen's shirt and then pulled him closer until his body was flush with hers. His lips tasted like fresh coffee, dark roast—her favorite—as all kinds of sensations lit her nerve endings on fire. Realizing her mouth was presently moving against Dillen's, she pulled back, wishing she could think of something snappy to say. Nothing came to mind because she'd wanted it to happen, too.

Taking in a deep breath only ushered in more of his spicy male scent. She chalked the kiss up to exhaustion. "That won't happen again."

"Good that you're not denying that you were a willing participant," he quipped, but she could tell by the huskiness in his voice the kiss had affected him more than he probably wanted to admit.

"No," she said. The infuriating part was that he might have started it, but she'd wanted it to happen just as much as he had. "But everyone has a lapse in judgment every once in a while. Doesn't mean it'll ever happen again." She balled her fist and then planted it on her hip. "Why don't you open the door so I can get some sleep. I must be delirious."

"Yes, ma'am," he said as he saluted. He was pushing her buttons, trying to get a reaction out of her.

Rather than go down that rabbit hole, she released a long, slow breath and then followed him to the door. The key was tucked underneath the mat—not exactly a secure place. Then again, folks out here didn't usually worry about security as much as those from a big city. Having a key at all was something.

Once inside, Dillen flipped on a light in the cozy living room. The place was clean. *Preserved* might've been a better word. There were plastic covers on the sofa and matching love seat. There weren't many decorations aside from matching lamps and several framed photos. The red brick fireplace had a wooden mantle painted white with several school photos of Dillen on top at various stages of childhood. Mr. Bullard had bought every grade and framed the five-by-sevens. It was sweet.

A rancid smell came from the kitchen area. Dillen immediately turned left and stomped over to investigate. His nose wrinkled as Liz pulled her shirt up over hers to buffer some of the odor.

Dillen muttered a curse after he opened the trash can lid. He immediately pulled the trash bag out and then closed it up. He held his arm out as he exited through the back door, propping it open, no doubt, to neutralize the smell as quickly as possible. She followed suit, turning on the vent over the stove before waving her arms in the air to dispel the stench.

Well, now she was awake.

Dillen joined her, opening windows. He grabbed a dish towel from the dishwasher handle and then waved it around. With the frigid temperatures and wind, the place was aired out in no time. Dillen replaced the trash bag with a new one before, one by one, closing the windows again. He left the one over the sink cracked.

"Sorry about that," he finally said. She couldn't be certain if he was referring to the smell or the kiss from earlier. Asking might've put them in territory she wasn't ready to explore. Plus, if it was the kiss, how awful would it be for someone to apologize after? She would have to be one terrible kisser for that to happen. Was she? Couldn't say she'd had any complaints up to now.

Get a grip. Liz's thoughts were spiraling because she was exhausted despite the recent surge of energy. Even so, she was running on fumes and didn't appreciate the timing of her second wind.

"Why don't you take the main bedroom?" Dillen asked. "My old room turned into a hobby room years ago."

When she lifted her eyes to meet his, she realized he'd been studying her.

"I don't think I could," she said. The thought of sleeping in Mr. Bullard's bed didn't sit right. Dillen might've been a class-A jerk, but his father had been nothing but kind to Liz. It didn't seem right to take over his room. "The couch looks comfy. Can we just throw a pillow and blanket over there?"

"Wouldn't you be more comfortable in a bed?"

Liz pushed away all thoughts of the word *bed* in the same sentence as Dillen. She was genuinely exhausted and standing upright solely due to a second wind as her thoughts kept circling back to the same topic…him. The man might've had a soft side—which he hid very well—and kissable lips, but that was no reason to keep thinking about him.

"I'll do fine on the sofa," she insisted. "Believe it or not, I won't find a pea under a mattress. I can sleep pretty much anywhere and have ever since business picked up. I can't tell you how many times I've fallen asleep with my head on my desk."

She was overexplaining, which didn't make sense, either. When had she started caring what Dillen Bullard thought about her?

"Have it your way," he said before disappearing into a back room. She assumed the main bedroom was there.

Examining the living room situation, she wondered if it would be all right to take the plastic covers off the furniture. The love seat was fine, as was the recliner that faced the TV, but she didn't want to make a crinkle noise every time she moved or sleep on top of plastic. It would get too hot. At least the smell was gone.

Liz bit back a yawn.

"Can I remove the couch cover?" she asked, shouting into the other room.

"Be my guest," came the response.

After taking the cover off, folding it and tucking

it away in the corner of the room, she moved to the kitchen, located a glass and filled it with water. On top of being slaphappy, she was thirsty.

The water helped ease some of the dryness in her throat. By the time she finished the drink, Dillen returned with folded up blankets stacked on his right shoulder and a pillow on top. He walked over to the couch and had it looking like a proper bed in the matter of a minute. The man had serious skills. How?

Right. The military.

How could she have forgotten, considering he had on fatigues?

Liz could admit Dillen Bullard had grown into a fine-looking man. She didn't remember much about him from school other than the fact he'd kept to himself. He'd been the only one who could climb the rope ladder in PE by the time high school had rolled around. That should have told her something about where he'd been headed.

"Thank you," she said as a wave of exhaustion struck. "Is there a place I can shower?"

"This way," Dillen said, leading her to a small hallway off the living room. There were three doors. Two on the left and one at the end of the hallway. "The first one here is the bathroom. The second one is my dad's home office, and the last one used to be where I slept when I was a kid that is now a hobby room." His chest was puffed out like he was prepared to take a punch. Did he really think so little of her that he believed she would judge a person for growing up in a trailer? The place had everything anyone would need to make a home.

Dillen opened the first door before taking a step inside. The bathroom had all the necessary equipment, including a stand-up shower. The floor creaked, and the bathmat was clean but worn. It looked original and was the color of dirt, but the whole color scheme was neutral, so it fit.

"Pop always kept toothbrushes from dentist trips in here," he said, opening a drawer in the cabinet. There were rows of toothbrushes, neatly lined up. "Feel free to use whatever you need."

She thanked him again, wishing her body didn't react every time he brushed past her.

DILLEN WASN'T READY to let Liz off the hook for being a snob just yet despite the fact she hadn't turned her nose up at the family trailer. He assumed she was silently judging his upbringing. Maybe the question was Why did he care? She was nobody to him and Pop. Well, that wasn't exactly true. She'd spent Pop's last moments with him despite not having a memory of what those had been.

After a good night of sleep, he intended to talk to her in the morning. He stepped out into the hallway. "Holler if you need anything. I'll drop a robe outside the door if you want to wash your clothes."

"Will do," she said, looking like she couldn't shut the door fast enough. "And thanks."

He walked into the living room and then grabbed the plastic wrapper she'd taken off the couch. He pulled the others off before folding them up. After depositing those in a closet, he wrangled a blanket. His rucksack had all the supplies he'd need to stay for the week while he handled Pop's affairs. Dillen had every intention of figuring out if foul play had been involved as Liz suspected.

He grabbed the robe while she showered, and then hooked it onto the door handle of the bathroom.

Rage heated the blood in his veins at the thought. His hands fisted at his sides. He flexed and released his fingers a couple of times to work off some of the tension before heading out to the Honda, where he'd left his rucksack in the back seat.

After retrieving his supplies, he scanned the area. Pop had lived on half an acre but owned the property behind his trailer, so there were no neighbors right on top of his place. There were several, smaller plots of land with trailers on his lane. Across the street and down a bit had a small plot of land where Rosa and Macy lived. They were sisters who looked in on Pop from time to time. The man had lived a simple life. He hadn't been wealthy. What could anyone have possibly wanted from him? Why would anyone have wanted to hurt him? Pop wouldn't have killed a bee, even if it had stung him. And he wouldn't go to the construction site on his own. Did someone lure him there? Drop him there?

Shouldering his rucksack, Dillen headed back inside. Liz was sitting on the couch.

"I'll be right back," he said, heading toward his father's bathroom.

Liz stood up and made a beeline for the door, locking it. Whatever had happened clearly had her riled up because folks didn't do that in these parts. It wasn't uncommon for someone to leave their keys in the drink holder, so they didn't have to carry them around, so locking their home wasn't normal behavior when there weren't many neighbors or main roads out here.

Dillen needed to get his bearings. Being back at the trailer without Pop had him off kilter. Memories engulfed him, threatening to suck him under and hold him there until he could no longer breathe. Since he hadn't slept in the main bedroom since he was five years old, and only when he'd had a bad dream, staying in there now was out of the question. He would rest in the recliner in the living room. Talk about memories. Glancing over at the bed now made his eyes water.

A quick shower later, he'd brushed his teeth and thrown on sweatpants and a cotton T-shirt. Normally he slept in boxers, but he didn't figure Liz would appreciate him walking around with almost no clothes on. Thinking about the kiss from earlier was enough to heat his blood. Bad idea. He didn't want something that had happened in a flash to occupy this much of his brain power. Still, he couldn't ignore the sizzle.

But Liz Hayes was off-limits. At the end of the day, she was a spoiled princess and Dillen's feet were firmly planted on the ground. They were from different worlds and had already clashed because of it. Right now, she was putting on a good show of being comfortable in the small trailer. How long could she keep it up?

On that note, he joined her in the living room and made himself comfortable on the recliner. She'd closed the window over the kitchen sink and was on her side, facing the room and softly snoring despite the lamp being on.

The warm glow from the microwave offered enough light for him to walk back over to the recliner without fear of stubbing his toe. Although he couldn't forget the layout since every piece of furniture sat in its exact same spot from the day it showed up.

Dillen let those thoughts carry him to sleep after he got comfortable on the recliner.

Not an hour later, wind howled loud enough to wake him. Liz sat bolt upright, searching the room as she clutched covers all the way up to her chest.

"It's just the wind," he said, rubbing his eyes with one hand as he searched for the recliner's lever with the other. His fingers curled around the wood before he tugged at it, causing the recliner to return to an upright position. He studied Liz to see if she was cognizant of what was happening or sitting up while still asleep. One of his buddies in his unit had a terrible habit of doing the same. He never spoke, just shot up to a sitting position in the middle of the night.

"You're okay." He tried to make his voice as soothing as possible, wondering if he was the last person on earth she wanted comforting her.

Liz nodded before crumpling onto her side again. Her eyelids fluttered before closing.

"Liz," he said quietly.

There was no response. The problem was he was awake. Going back to sleep would be impossible, but he'd gotten in a solid forty-five minutes. He'd survived on less sleep for longer amounts of time. Then again, since hearing the news Pop was in the hospital, he hadn't really slept.

What the hell was he supposed to do while he sat there? Making noise might wake Liz. She needed sleep. No, she deserved sleep.

Pop had a desktop computer in his home office. Dillen could start there and poke around to see if he found anything suspicious.

Dillen threw the covers off. He knew exactly where to step so the floor wouldn't creak underneath his weight. The wind, however, had a mind of its own. It howled, shaking the double wide. He stopped half-way across the room mid-step.

Liz's steady breathing said she was still asleep. Good.

He crossed the room and entered the hallway without making a sound. The door to Pop's office was closed. Dillen stood there, holding on to the door handle, unable to make his hand move. He leaned his shoulder against the door and then the side of his head.

Why was walking inside harder than any mission he'd ever been on?

Chapter Five

The walls shook, causing Liz to sit bolt upright. She glanced around the room, trying to gain her bearings. Nothing looked familiar.

Shaking her head to break through the fog, she remembered. Dillen had brought her here to rest before they dissected what had actually happened to his father and why she'd woken up in a hospital after stopping at an intersection during a freak ice storm. A weather system had been moving in, and she'd heard cries for help, or so she'd been told.

The recliner had a blanket draped over it. Where was Dillen?

Liz stretched her arms out and released a yawn. She pushed to standing, got a little woozy and almost immediately sat right back down. She took a minute to regroup and heard clicking noises coming from down the hall. Was Dillen on the computer?

The second attempt at standing produced far better results. She took a couple of steps toward the hallway, and the flooring creaked underneath her weight.

"I'm in here," Dillen said. His masculine voice

slid over her and through her despite her best efforts to reject it. Goose bumps formed on her arms as she thought about what else those lips of his were good for. This seemed like a good time to remind herself that she wasn't here for a social call. No matter how hot the man was, he was off-limits. Not that she needed to worry, considering the only reason he was able to be in the same room with her was to find answers about his father's death. Murder?

Liz took in a deep breath. *Murder* was a strong word. And yet it resonated.

Had Mr. Bullard said something to her? She pushed for answers but only managed to cause an ache to form in the spot right between her eyes.

After issuing a sharp sigh, she headed toward the clicking sound of fingers on a keyboard. Another deep breath later, she walked inside the office. The room had a desk pushed up against the wall to her right. There was a plastic floor mat underneath a leather chair on wheels, taking up much of the middle of the room. A framed American flag along with a picture of a young Dillen in his army uniform was on the wall. And then another picture of him in salute as a Green Beret, which she recognized as the army's Special Forces soldiers. An old metal filing cabinet that stood five feet tall was pushed up against the left back corner of the room.

"Did the wind wake you up again?" Dillen asked, nodding toward the chair in the corner next to the desk.

"Again?" she parroted.

"I thought you might have been asleep last time," he said as he stared at the monitor. "The wind was something last night."

Liz took a seat, perching on the edge of the chair, and yawned. "I have no recollection of being awake before, but I'll take your word for it."

"Are you hungry?" he asked, his tone and demeanor much softer than last night. Then again, he deserved a break considering he'd just learned the news his father was gone.

"Maybe in a few minutes," she said. "I'm currently in that sleep-fog where it feels like you're moving outside your body."

He nodded before clicking the tab closed and then swiveling the chair around toward her. He leaned forward and clasped his hands together. "I had no idea there would be so many decisions to make after…"

"My grandfather died a few months back, and I bet my mother is still drowning in paperwork," she admitted.

"You don't know for certain?" he asked with a cocked eyebrow.

"I run my own business, so, no, I haven't been home or checking in much," she said by way of explanation. It was a cop-out, but she wasn't quite ready to examine the reasoning.

Dillen opened his mouth to speak, but she cut him off. "By the way, Hayes family members work their backsides off making their own businesses, so don't look so surprised that I built one from the ground up."

His questioning expression morphed into a small smile. "Sorry. Note taken."

"It's just you seemed to be confusing me with some entitled princess last night, and reality couldn't be further from it," she continued while she had his ear.

The smile widened, and she didn't want to notice how full his lips were or how much more attractive the man was when he smiled.

He opened his mouth to speak again before clamping his lips shut.

"What?" she asked. "Did you have something to add?"

"Are you finished?" he asked with that bemused smile planted on lips that covered perfectly white and almost perfectly straight teeth.

A solid reason for that statement being infuriating to her wasn't readily available, but there she was angry anyway. And then it came to her. It was the tone more than the words. Mocking?

"I'm just saying that you were a jerk last night," she defended, hugging her arms across her chest.

"Hey, that's personal," he teased, tensing up like he'd just taken a punch.

"Dillen, can we be serious for a minute?" she broke down and asked on an exhale.

"Yes, ma'am," he said, sitting up a little straighter and removing the smile.

"Good," she said.

"Before you say anything else, I do recognize that you are here out of the goodness of your heart, prince—"

She shot him a look that stopped him cold.

"Liz," he corrected. "And I do appreciate the fact you stayed with Pop…not to mention the fact you're here now trying to help sort this out. I was going on emotion last night and probably a few preconceived notions about you. No matter what, I had no right. I'd like to offer an apology if you're willing to accept it."

"Done," she said, studying him. His demeanor had softened, or maybe it was just his face muscles that looked less tense. In fact, a deep sadness set in his eyes that formed an ache in her chest. Kindred spirits? "Now we can get down to business."

An emotion flashed behind his eyes now that she didn't want to analyze because it looked a whole lot like desire. Couldn't be, though. Dillen Bullard could barely stand the ground she walked on. Clearly.

But she wasn't here for him. She felt bad for Mr. Bullard. The sweet older man hadn't deserved what had happened to him.

"We have to go back there," she said. "To the site, so I can retrace my steps and maybe get a memory or two back of what actually happened." She would prefer to remember everything, but what if her brain was protecting her from information so horrific that knowing would cause nightmares or a major depression? Fear? Should she be afraid that whoever tried to kill her would come back to finish the job?

For Mr. Bullard's sake, she needed to know what had happened.

"Okay," Dillen said. "I'll be right there with you in

case the bastard or bastards who did this to you and Pop come back."

Did he sense her fears? A highly person trained like him would probably be able to read someone with one look.

Or maybe a better question would be to ask why she cared what he thought in the first place.

DILLEN'S AMUSEMENT FADED the second he realized Liz was afraid to go back to the site on her own. Being here in the home where he'd grown up probably wasn't high on the list of places she wanted to visit. He needed to remember that and hold his tongue on the sharp digs. Being glued to her meant finding out what really happened to his father. This was his new mantra. It would keep him focused on what was important instead of slipping into the past. And besides, he appreciated her help.

Somewhere locked inside her brain might've been the key to figuring out what had really happened. Dillen had only so much time on leave. Time was of the essence.

"Thank you," she said on an exhale. "I wish I could remember." She brought her hands up to rub her temples. "All I get is a headache and no answers."

"You've been through a lot," he said, trying his best to find a way to reassure her. "Don't be too hard on yourself."

She nodded. The acknowledgment followed by the look of relief in her eyes shouldn't have caused his chest to swell with pride as much as it did.

"It's frustrating to feel like I might have answers locked away inside here," she admitted.

"I imagine it is," he said. "Trust the memories will come back. Do your best not to fixate on them."

"Okay," she said. "I'll do my best. Relaxing isn't exactly my forte."

"Can I ask a question?" One had been burning in the back of his mind.

"Sure."

"Why not call your family to stay at the hospital with you?" he asked.

"How do you know I didn't?" she asked, her eyebrow shooting up.

"They would have still been there," he said. "You guys were like a clan in school, always protecting one another and having each other's backs."

"They brought food, but we didn't always get along when we were younger," she pointed out. "There were four strong-willed boys in the house along with me and my sister."

"Only child," he said on a shrug.

"Then let me fill you in," she said. "My brothers and sister might have had my back, but they were also pains in the neck. No one could talk to me or about me when they were within earshot."

"I could see why they might've wanted to protect you against high school boys," he said. "Most of the ones in our school were all testosterone and little brains."

"It didn't seem to matter that I could handle myself," she continued. "I'm pretty certain they threatened anyone who got within five feet of me."

"Never thought about it like that," he said. It could explain why she'd been so standoffish back in school. She hadn't wanted her brothers interrogating anyone.

"High school was a lonely time," she said. The admission surprised him given her family's popular status.

"The teachers had high expectations of me being a Hayes," she said. "I couldn't step out of line in the slightest."

He hadn't thought about the pressure that might come with a famous last name. Then again, he'd had bigger fish to fry. Like being able to keep food on the table in his youth. His father's paycheck had barely covered essentials, not that Dillen should complain. Looking back, Pop had done the best he could with what he had to work with. "Living under a microscope couldn't have been fun."

"It was miserable," she said. "Why do you think I bolted the day after graduation like my siblings?"

"You moved away from Cider Creek?" he asked, incredulous. His jaw shouldn't have dropped, but it did. Why would a princess like Liz leave town? Because a few people had kept an eye on her every move? When he heard himself say it like that, it didn't sound great. In fact, it felt stifling.

"Why does that surprise you so much?" she asked with more than a little indignation in his tone. Fair.

"I just realized what you were saying, and it sounds like its own hell to be a Hayes in this town." He wasn't one hundred percent on board with changing his opinions, but he was starting to see that her last name could have been an albatross around her neck.

"Honestly, I had a roof over my head and food on the table," she said. "My mother and Granny loved us, and they did the best they could after my father died. The fact that Duncan Hayes existed to make our lives a living hell shouldn't taint everything good."

Dillen had forgotten about the fact her father had died when she was young. He also hadn't thought about how terrible it might've been to live under the iron fist of Duncan Hayes. His image in Cider Creek might have been as town savior, but Dillen had never liked the man. Was he beginning to see Liz in a different light?

"Your grandfather was a piece of work," he agreed.

"You better believe it," she snapped. "What happened at home didn't fit the good family man image he portrayed in public. But how did you see it when no one else in town seemed to?"

"I was never enamored by all of his donations and money," he said point-blank.

"Good that someone in town could see through him," she said. It was the first time he realized her disdain for Duncan Hayes might've been on par with his. "I shouldn't speak ill of the dead, but the only positive that I got from my grandfather was his work ethic."

"At least something good came from being related to the man," he conceded, figuring a trust fund was probably another benefit. All grown up, she didn't fit the trust-fund bill. There wasn't anything about her that said she was lazy or entitled like he imagined most rich kids were. He wouldn't know firsthand because he didn't hang out with trust-fund babies. In fact, this was the closest he'd ever been to one.

"Working on a ranch didn't exactly jive with manicured nails or high heels," she continued, like she had something to prove. He should know. He recognized the defense mechanism since it was his go-to.

Damn. Was he admitting the two of them might be alike in some way?

Dillen sat up a little straighter, rejecting the idea before it took hold. Liz Hayes didn't need anyone's pity, especially not his. So why was he softening toward her?

Chapter Six

Liz's stomach growled. "I guess I'm hungrier than I realized."

"Let's get something to eat," Dillen said, immediately standing. He waited for her as she pushed up, got a little woozy and then pulled it together. "You need food, but I can't make any promises."

"I'd eat crackers at this point," she admitted. The thought of coffee had her feet moving faster toward the kitchen. Could she, though? Would caffeine make her headache worse or better? It dawned on her that caffeine might actually solve her headache. She hadn't had a cup in days. "I saw a coffee maker on the counter."

"Coffee is guaranteed in this house," he said as they cut across the living room and walked into the kitchen.

The pantry was stocked. Overstocked, in fact.

"It's not like Pop to have more than he needed for a week," Dillen said as he appraised the cabinet. There had to be five bags of coffee grounds, all the same dark-roast flavor. "This isn't like him."

"Your father liked his routines," she said. "I'm guessing shopping is one of many."

Dillen nodded. "He doesn't—*didn't*—do anything out of the ordinary. Stocking up on supplies like coffee doesn't make sense."

"Here, let's check the expiration dates," she offered. "Maybe he just didn't like to throw anything away."

They checked each bag one by one. The dates were all similar, meaning the coffee had been bought at roughly the same time.

"Pop must have been off lately," he deduced. "Maybe his memory was starting to fade."

She opened the fridge. "Did he normally drink wine?"

"Pop? No," he said as he turned around. His gaze landed hard on the half-empty bottle in the fridge along with several unopened bottles in the door. Dillen scratched his head. "I have no idea when this started."

"Was it possible he was dating someone?" she asked.

"No, but then I didn't think he drank wine or stocked up on coffee, either," he admitted with a shrug. "I'm in new territory here."

Her mind immediately snapped to Mr. Bullard dating a married woman. Weren't passion killings one of the top reasons for murder? "What about a new friend?"

"That I do not know," he said. "Again, I would have said no to that question before. In all my years growing up here, the man never once went on a date or brought home a buddy to watch a game or have a beer."

"You joined the military and left home," she pointed out. "Is it possible he was lonely?"

Dillen shrugged. "Anything is possible at this point. Is it probable? I don't think so. But what do I know?" He issued a sharp sigh. "TV used to be company enough for him. Believe me when I say he watched certain shows every night my entire childhood."

"What would cause him to change his routine?" she asked.

"That's the sixty-four-thousand-dollar question." Dillen grabbed coffee before closing the cabinet. "Do you see anything edible in the fridge?"

"The eggs haven't expired," she said before opening the freezer. "I can use these tater tots to make something that resembles hash browns."

"Sounds like a plan," he said as he went to work on a pot of coffee. There were no fancy pods. Just a good old reliable Mr. Coffee machine that had been around since the dawn of time. Filters were not in short supply, either.

Had Mr. Bullard been sick? Was that the reason he'd stockpiled? Had he been dating?

Questions piled up as she pulled out the ingredients to make breakfast. The milk was fresh, so she poured a glass to calm her stomach before whipping up fried eggs and makeshift hash browns.

"I'm surprised a Hayes knows how to cook," Dillen said, breaking the good vibes they'd had going while working together in the kitchen.

This time, she let the comment roll right off her. If he was trying to get a rise out of her, it wouldn't work.

The eggs came out nicely, as did the hash browns. Before she could ask for a plate, two appeared next to the stove on the counter. She could feel Dillen's masculine presence without glancing in his direction. The man was also stealthy, so he was out of the way pouring coffee before she had a chance to thank him for the plates.

After dividing up the food, she brought the dishes over to the table. Dillen brought mugs and then silverware.

"Smells good," he practically grunted. Was he upset with her for not responding to his dig? He'd corrected himself, but it was clear his impression of her and her family was the same despite her opening up about what life was really like for her growing up a Hayes. So be it. She wanted answers to who would have wanted to murder a kind older man like Mr. Bullard. Secondly, she needed to know if someone was coming after her. And third, she didn't want to care why Dillen's opinion mattered so much to her.

They'd shared one good kiss. It barely qualified, and yet her heart argued the opposite. Her lips still sizzled from the contact. Even though their lips had barely touched, this would be the new benchmark for every future kiss.

"What kind of work do you do?" Dillen broke the silence.

"I run an accessory business over the internet,"

she supplied, figuring that was enough information for him to stop asking questions.

"Does that mean jewelry?" he asked.

"No," she stated before stabbing a piece of tater tot with her fork. She took a bite and then chewed. Since talking about her personal life hadn't gone so well earlier, she didn't plan to go there again.

"Are any other memories coming back?" he asked, breaking eye contact.

"I wish I did," she said. "All I keep thinking is that your dad didn't deserve what happened to him."

"We're in agreement there," he said. "I should check out his bathroom a little closer to see if there's any hint of a woman having been here."

"They might have gone to her place," she offered.

"True," he agreed. "Plus, Pop would have cleaned up right after she left here, so there won't likely be any traces left behind."

"We could ask neighbors," she said.

Dillen snapped his fingers. "You know what? I remember seeing one of Pop's neighbors at the hospital. Mr. Martin. We should definitely drive around and ask questions. I don't know the guy very well. It's not like we had neighborhood parties or broke out the grill. Pop kept to himself mostly, but there was a man…"

"Wish I could help with names, but I haven't lived in Cider Creek in forever," she said.

"I doubt you made it over to this side of the tracks much anyway," he commented.

Later today she would think of a great zinger in response. But right now, nothing came to mind. Why did that always happen? The minute she laid her head down on the pillow at night, she thought of every great comeback. But now? Speechless.

THE LAST THING Dillen needed was to get close to a Hayes. They couldn't be trusted, no matter how soft their skin was or how sincere those eyes were.

"All done?" he asked, figuring his contribution to the meal would be clearing the table and throwing the dishes into the dishwasher.

"Yes," Liz said with a back stiffer than a corpse.

He cleared the table as she sat and sipped from her coffee mug. The meal had been good. Better than good. He'd been utterly shocked a Hayes could pull off a decent breakfast. Didn't they all have hired help even as adults?

"I doubt you guys have the work ethic of ranchers on this side of the tracks, but I imagine most folks rise with the sun," Liz said after taking another sip.

Shots fired.

Dillen cracked a smile because her zinger was a good one.

"The neighbors should be up," he said. "They're good folks. You should pop over here and get to know how the other half lives."

"Really? Why would I do that when I can hang out with one percenters all day?" she asked dismissively.

The caffeine must've been kicking in was all he could think because her comebacks were getting snappier each time. The banter proved she wasn't a complete uptight princess.

"Good point," he said before placing the last dish in the machine. "I'll try to remember that when I'm throwing my next hoedown."

Liz laughed. The sound was like music filling the air.

"I have brothers who gave me a hard time growing up," she said by way of explanation. "And I don't normally get insulted by the opposite sex, but I haven't spoken to them in years other than an occasional text check-in, so I'm rusty with the insults."

He had to give it to her. She was taking his jabs better than he expected for a spoiled trust-fund baby. "They trained you well."

"A lifetime with four brothers should do something besides drive me up the wall," she commented, rolling her eyes. "You would probably get along with them pretty well."

"I doubt it," he said reflexively.

"Why?"

"They never spoke a word to me in high school. Why would they start now?" he asked, hearing the defensiveness in his own voice.

"They didn't know you back then," she said. "As memory serves, you were in my grade."

"That's right."

"Were they awful to you?" she asked.

"No. Can't say they were," he responded.

"Okay, then I guess I don't understand why you hate us so much," she stated with a raised eyebrow.

"Duncan Hayes," he said, surprised by his own honesty.

"That makes sense to me," she quipped. "But I'm not sure why you think it's a good idea to judge the whole family based on one person's actions. We're all different, and no one disliked Duncan Hayes more than me and my siblings."

"Is that why you didn't go straight home from the hospital or call your family?" he asked, using the mention of her grandfather to switch topics.

"I'm not ready to face them until I've figured out what happened to Mr. Bullard," she said honestly. "My family is a whole thing that sucks you in." She shook her head. "Once I step inside the door, I'll be sucked in."

"Everyone knows your family, right?" he asked.

"Just about everyone," she responded. "Though, to be honest, I haven't been home in so long I doubt anyone would recognize me."

"Despite more than a decade passing since you were last here, you haven't changed a bit."

"Oh, I've changed," she countered with a grunt of disapproval. "I'm not at all the scared kid that I used to be."

Dillen studied her as the dots seemed to be connecting in her brain. She frowned.

"I should probably call them again to let them know I made it here," she said on a sigh.

"I'm surprised they haven't blown up your phone already," he admitted.

"They respect my wishes," she said. "Since I didn't reach out to them, they'll assume I want space. Plus, they're busy with their own lives and work."

"Doesn't sound like the same group who wouldn't let a guy get close to you in high school," he said.

"Like I said, we've all grown up since then," she defended. "You're not exactly the same tall, skinny kid I remember, either."

"I'm surprised you noticed me at all," he quipped. He'd changed since high school in more ways than he could count, and yet one thing had remained a constant. Anger. The military had given him better coping mechanisms for it. But it had never subsided. The fact that Pop was gone struck like a physical blow, exploding inside his body with nowhere for it to exit. No release. Now all that anger balled inside him, forming a hard knot in the center of his chest.

Dillen issued a sharp sigh. Going down that road always led to the same result. More frustration.

"Come on," she said. "Our school wasn't that big. You might have always kept to yourself, but that didn't mean I wouldn't have talked to you if you'd seem the least bit interested in a conversation."

"I'm pretty sure everyone wanted your attention," he said. "But you always sat alone. I'm guessing it has more to do with what you wanted versus your brothers being overprotective."

"I won't lie. High school was brutal," she admitted, catching him off guard.

"Even for a princess like you?" he asked, immediately regretting his word choice. Words meant to mask the simple fact that he wanted to kiss her like they'd invented the idea.

Chapter Seven

Dillen Bullard was infuriating. His opinion would never change, so why bother correcting him again?

Liz stood, crossed her arms over her chest and tapped her toe on the vinyl flooring in the kitchen. "I'm ready if you want to go speak to the neighbors and then visit the construction site together."

He glanced out of the curtain over the kitchen window and nodded. "It didn't dawn on me last night that Pop's car is here."

"Could mean he was taken from here to the site," she reasoned.

"Or that he went for a walk and was grabbed," he said.

"True," she said, taking a mental note of the recent supply hoarding activities. The rest of Mr. Bullard's trailer was just like usual according to Dillen, who'd disappeared into the main bedroom after excusing himself and mumbling something about throwing a sweater on.

The wind had calmed down, and it wasn't raining. The weather conditions might have had an impact on the construction site. A growing piece of her wanted to swing by there first before evidence could be blown away by the wind if it hadn't already. As heavy as those winds were last night, debris might have been tossed around, too.

Liz had been in the hospital for five days. Today counted six since the so-called accident. Again, she wondered why Mr. Bullard would've been wandering around during an ice storm. Wouldn't he have driven? His home was on the outskirts of town, too far to walk. He hadn't seemed to be a runner. She didn't figure he'd changed his habits.

Dillen entered the room as he pulled a sweater on over his head.

"I've never seen your father run," she said.

"Pop? No," he confirmed. "That's because he didn't exercise other than walk. I bought weights and put a bench out in the shed but never could convince him to use them. He didn't like workouts and could be as stubborn as a mule when he didn't want to do something."

"The site is far from here," she continued. "I'm wondering how he got there if his car is still here. Did he ride a bike?"

He shook his head. "He wouldn't have taken one out in bad weather even if he did own one, and there was no getting him on the back of a motorcycle. Believe me, I tried once. It was a disaster."

"Was he ever diagnosed as autistic?" she asked.

"No," he said. "Not that I'm aware of."

"So, you don't know exactly what you're dealing with?" she asked.

"He was different," Dillen said with fire in his eyes. "He liked his routines more than most. It's no different than me being in the military. I've seen guys who thrive on routine, waking up at five thirty every morning so they can go through the same motions every day. Doesn't mean they need a diagnosis."

"Okay," she said, realizing she'd just hit on a sore spot. "I wasn't saying there was anything wrong with your father."

Dillen moved to the coffee maker, poured another cup and then turned off the machine. "Do you want more before we head out?"

"No, thanks," she said, realizing a wall had just come up between them. "I've had enough for one morning."

Her statement covered more than she planned to discuss right now.

"Do you want to go to the construction site first?" she asked. "I was thinking the longer we wait the colder the crime scene becomes."

"The neighbors can wait," he said before throwing a couple of ice cubes into the mug. After stirring, he drained the contents. "If we find anything, we go to the sheriff and ask him to open a criminal case."

Good. The thought of revisiting the crime scene, if it could be called that, had her nerves on edge. A growing part of her wanted to face it and get it over with. Right now, her hands were trembling at the thought of going back there. At the thought of what she might find. And at the thought of what she might remember.

Anticipation was the absolute worst. At this point, she needed to get the visit over with even if it stirred up a flood of memories she couldn't handle. Correction, she would find a way to cope with whatever came her way. She always did. History would repeat itself, and she would find a way to deal.

Again, the thought her brain might be protecting her from something potentially devastating hit her.

You got this.

If she could leave home after graduation at eighteen years old, survive on her own and start a successful business, she could handle anything.

After putting on her coat and shoes, she walked out to her Honda with Dillen. "Do you mind driving?"

Dillen said he didn't before opening the door for her and then claiming the driver's seat for himself. "I almost thought about taking out Pop's vehicle. I don't know how many folks know about his passing. The grapevine is strong in these parts, if memory serves."

"It sure used to be," she said. "Couldn't tell you what has changed since I last lived here considering next year marks my fifteenth year away from Cider Creek."

"You really hated it that bad?" he asked as he navigated onto the roadway.

"Couldn't wait to get out, and never looked back," she admitted. "So, yes, you could say that it wasn't my cup of tea."

The rest of the drive to the construction site was spent in quiet contemplation. Every muscle in Liz's body tensed a little more as they neared the intersection. It was the last place in her memory of that night.

She located her cell inside her purse and then sent a text to her oldest brother, Callum, letting him know where she was and what she was up to. He'd stepped into the role of family caregiver after their dad had died despite how much she'd fought him on it.

A response came back almost immediately. Come home when UR ready. B Careful.

"All good," she said out loud as she responded with a thank U. Thinking back, she'd always been able to talk to Callum. Then there was her younger sister, Reese, a sister who'd just decided to get married according to the sibling group chat.

In fact, all of her siblings had found love and happiness right here in or near Cider Creek upon their return. The last thing Liz needed to complicate her life was a relationship. She shuttered thinking about how possessive her last boyfriend had become when she couldn't tear herself away from a business that was flying high. She'd worked too hard to get where she was to have anyone derail her. Having to choose between a man and the business she'd built from the ground up had been a no-brainer.

The right man would understand her well enough to know better than to draw a line in the sand. Hell, he'd even support her rather than complain that making a living was taking too much time away from the relationship.

"Do they want you to come home?" he asked. She

noticed he gripped the steering wheel a little tighter when he asked the question.

"When I'm ready," she said. "Callum understands." And then it dawned on her that her sister was marrying one of Dillen's old friends. "I'm guessing you already know this, but Reese and Darren are getting married."

"Darren Pierce?" he asked.

The incredulous note to his tone put her off.

"What? You don't think my sister is good enough to marry him?" she asked.

"I never thought he'd end up with a Hayes, if that's what you're asking," he said like it should've been a known fact.

"You may not like my family but, you know, not everyone automatically hates us because my grandfather was a jerk," she quipped. "Some folks actually give us the benefit of the doubt."

"Everyone sucked up to your grandfather," he responded.

"Clearly not *everyone*."

DARREN NEEDED TO have his head examined for getting romantically involved with a Hayes after it hadn't worked out the first time, as far as Dillen was concerned. Darren and Liz Hayes had been high school sweethearts years ago before she broke his heart, left town and didn't look back. Dillen hadn't thought about his old friend in years. Back in high school, teachers used to mix the two of them up based on their names despite the fact they'd looked nothing alike. The similarities ended with the alphabet. Their taste in women couldn't have been more different, even though Dillen could admit to feeling a pull toward Liz like nothing he'd ever experienced in the past.

That wasn't entirely true. He'd had a severe crush on her during high school, and those old feelings must've been resurfacing now. If someone had told seventeen-year-old him that he would kiss Liz Hayes at some point in the future, he might have laughed. Or punched them. Thankfully, he'd gotten a tighter grip on his anger since then.

Liz's cell phone buzzed. He caught her staring at the screen out of the corner of his eye.

"The family meeting is being put on hold indefinitely," she said to him. "And my sister is asking how you're doing, so I guess the whole town knows we're spending time together."

"What meeting?" he asked.

"One my mother called to discuss next steps with the family ranch," she said. "Now that Duncan is gone and a little time has passed, I imagine she wants to know where we stand on the family business."

The cell buzzed again before he had a chance to respond.

"Everyone sends their condolences and wants to know if there's anything you need," she continued. "Darren doesn't have your contact information any longer, or he would reach out himself."

Well, damn. He'd be a jerk to pop off at the mouth when people were offering sympathy. He wasn't.

And, honestly, he appreciated their sentiment. Now that Pop was gone, Darren had no family left to speak of. His mother had ditched when he'd been a kid, too young to remember her. He had no siblings that he knew of. He'd grown up an only child who'd learned to depend on himself from an early age.

"Tell them I appreciate their offer," he said, stopping himself before saying he was fine. He wasn't fine. In fact, he'd never been less fine in his life. "If I think of anything, I'll reach out."

She nodded and typed on the screen.

"Can I give them your cell number?" she asked.

"Why not," he said, glancing up at the sky to see if pigs were flying. There was a time when he'd believed he would witness that before he'd be in contact with a Hayes. Maybe he should start believing in miracles after all. He fished his cell phone out of his pocket before handing it over.

Liz took it, and their fingers grazed. He didn't want to think about the jolt of electricity or the tension that seemed to sit thickly between them, charging the air. She immediately looked away from him after taking the offering and intensely focused on the screen.

"Mind if I put you in my contacts?" she asked without looking up.

"No, go ahead," he said. "Do you mind making sure I have your information?"

"Sure," she said after clearing her throat.

Dillen pulled up to the construction site. The sun was shining, which made the forty-eight-degree temperatures feel a whole lot warmer inside the vehicle. They would be hit with the cold again the second they opened the doors.

After taking in a deep breath, Liz shifted her gaze from the phones. He sat with her car idling at the same red light she'd mentioned, but they were coming from the opposite side. Her mind was blocking out the memories. Protecting her? He wanted to do the same, even though he realized bringing her here to get answers might create more stress.

It was an impossible situation. He could shield her from this place and, possibly, keep her from remembering. Or he could confine his anger and help her face whatever came next. Since he didn't intend to let her out of his sight until they found answers, he had no choice but to walk her through this place.

"Let me know whenever you're ready," he said, idling the engine at the light. "Take your time."

"I came from the opposite side of the street," she said, pointing. "It was getting hard to see out of my front windshield while I sat at the light because the cold front came in so quickly. Everything started fogging up, so I rolled down my window. That's when I heard a noise." She flashed eyes at him. "I thought it sounded like a wounded animal."

A coil tightened in his chest at thinking of his father being left out here alone to die.

"The last thing I remember is getting out of my vehicle and running toward the sound," she said before pinching the bridge of her nose. There was still a bandage on her head. She would need to follow up with the doctor at some point. "This is so frustrating. My head hurts when I focus on recall too much. It's like the next few minutes of what happened are locked inside a vault in my brain and I can't break in no matter how hard I try. In fact, trying seems to make it worse."

"It'll be all right," he soothed, reaching for her hand while readying himself for the now-familiar jolt. "We'll find answers. I promise you."

It was a promise he intended to keep even if it killed him.

"Are you ready to park?" he asked when she didn't respond.

Her lips curled down at the edges, frowning. "We can't sit here forever. This might be a small town, but someone will come roaring up here eventually."

It dawned on him that someone might have come up on the scene during the ice storm. Then again, folks hunkered down in times like those, not wanting to venture out into the streets past dark. Towns like Cider Creek shut down as soon as the sun dropped below the horizon. Plus, it was the holidays, so workers would have been sent home. Most construction sites in small towns were staffed with out of town folks.

"We can take it slow," he said. "Other people will have to get over themselves if they show up here."

Liz squeezed his hand. "Thank you. That means a lot."

Those words shouldn't have made him want to open his heart to her. But they did.

Chapter Eight

The compassionate side to Dillen wasn't something Liz was used to. It made him even more attractive. She didn't need to be more attracted to him, so she shut down her feelings, let go of his hand and threw up a boundary. Dillen Bullard was off-limits. It would be a mistake to lean into his comfort. Because he would leave town once he'd handled his father's affairs and she would never see the man again. She needed to keep their interactions in perspective, which wasn't something she was used to forcing. Normally, it came naturally.

Being here at the site wasn't helping with her memory, so they needed to hunt for clues. "I think it's safe to pull onto the side of the road and park."

Dillen did as requested. His change in demeanor was nice.

He was on her side of the Honda in a matter of seconds, opening the door for her and offering a hand up. She accepted the help, doing her best to ignore the way his touch made her feel and all the senses he awakened in her.

Walking around the Honda…there was still nothing. No memory of what had happened after exiting her vehicle at the light. Construction seemed to have stopped. Was it the weather or the holidays?

Looking down, she retraced what might have been her steps. The freezing rain had helped with footprints on the cold, unforgiving earth. She followed a trail that looked like it might have been her shoe size.

The case was dismissed as an accident, and yet everything inside her screamed this was anything but. Getting the law to believe her considering she had memory loss was another story altogether.

"Are you okay?" Dillen asked. She appreciated the fact he was checking in with her.

"So far," she said. "But I'm frustrated as all getout that I can't remember. I feel so close to the information. It's almost taunting me."

"Have faith in yourself," he said. "Relax, if at all possible. It'll come back."

She took those words to heart, wishing they were true. "What if it doesn't? What if I can't remember?" A few beats passed. "What if I'm the reason you have no closure on your father's murder?"

"Then we'll find the answers another way," he admitted. "Your memory is only one possibility. We have others. We have the crime scene, for starters. This is significant."

He was right. So, why wasn't she ready to let herself forgive herself?

Was it because she'd always taken everything personally?

Liz took in a breath and regrouped. Focusing on work was so much easier than dealing with the real world. Had she been hiding, like her last boyfriend had suggested?

Well, hell. She wasn't here to solve her personal problems. She'd come here to find a murderer.

"Those are my footprints," she said. "Watch this." She took a step beside one of the prints. The imprint was a perfect match.

"Let's follow your walking pattern, then," he said, hot on the trail. They walked past the porta potty, and around a cone before stopping in front of a stack of Sheetrock that towered over both of them. "Look at this."

He pointed toward an area that looked like a body had been pulled out from underneath a stack of Sheetrock. An image scorched her brain. A trembling hand. A cry for help.

A gasp escaped before she covered her mouth with her hand to suppress it. "I remember this."

After telling Dillen what she recalled, he stood there quiet, studying the area.

"Look at this," he said, pointing toward footsteps walking away from the area. There were two distinct sets of tracks. "The frozen ground kept the prints intact. These should be work boots, but they're not."

"Those tips look like cowboy boots," she agreed.

"Not the usual footwear for a job site," he continued. Were they onto something big? Something that could break this case wide open?

It felt right. And then unfamiliar voices stirred

in her memory bank. They were muffled. It was almost like trying to listen to someone in a tunnel, just out of reach. "No, it isn't. Why would anyone wear cowboy boots?"

"There are two sets of tracks here," he continued, clearly on a trail. He followed them to where they stopped. "It looks like whatever they were carrying got dropped right here."

The imprint in the earth seemed to agree with his assessment.

"I hear voices in the back of my head," she said. "Male, and at least two of them. But I can't make them out."

"Meaning you don't recognize them?" he asked.

"Right, but then I haven't been home in fourteen years," she said.

"Do you think you would be able to identify them if you heard them again?" he asked.

"It's possible," she said. "I'm not getting anything clearly right now, though. I'd be guessing, which could implicate an innocent man, and there's no way I could live with myself if I pinned the wrong person to a crime like murder."

"Or you might lead the sheriff's office in the right direction," he said, pulling out his cell phone and taking pictures of the site.

"The cowboy boot prints leave in this direction," she said, following the trail. "There are men-size tennis shoe imprints going back the other way."

"I'm guessing these belong to the EMTs on the

scene," he said, motioning toward the footprints. "And these could belong to a deputy or the sheriff."

"A gurney probably wouldn't be able to roll across this terrain, so they would have carried your father," she continued before making eye contact with Dillen. "I remember a hand coming out of this pile of broken Sheetrock. And then another cry for help."

Her heart ached at the look on his face at hearing his father had been abandoned, left to die and in pain. His hands fisted at his sides, and tension rolled off him in palpable waves.

"I'm so sorry," she said, hating to be the one who put the look there. "He didn't deserve this." A rogue tear escaped, running down her cheek.

Dillen's hand came up immediately before thumbing the tear away. He dropped his balled fist to rest on her shoulder. She took a step toward him, closing the distance between them.

Their gazes locked, and she knew in an instant her heart was in trouble. Doing her best to set personal feelings aside, she leaned into Dillen. His strong arms looped around her waist as she buried her head in his chest, unable and unwilling to maintain eye contact when she was this close to him.

Besides, she wanted to be here for him in what must've been one of the worst moments of his life. Facing down the spot where his father's life had been essentially snubbed out practically gutted her, so she could only imagine the effect it was having on Dillen.

"Your father was a good man," she said when she could finally find her voice. "He didn't deserve this."

"I know," he said, his voice husky and raw with emotion—emotion removed from all anger. In that moment, he was just a man, not a seasoned soldier, who was trying to cope with unimaginable loss.

"We'll figure this out," she said, stopping herself before saying the word *together*. When they were standing with bodies flush, heat flooding her, she needed to stay as far away from that word as possible. It was dangerous to think it, let alone speak it out loud.

"I hope so," came the response. There was a desperation in his tone like she'd never heard from the normally arrogant-to-the-point-of-almost-cocky man. She reminded herself that underneath all the anger was a human, just like everyone else. Dillen was hurting, his heart broken, and he was letting down his guard for what she was certain would be a few brief moments.

He needed to know someone cared. Cared about his father. Cared about the murder. And cared about Dillen.

"He wouldn't have gone out. Thursday is always TV night," Dillen said, his voice still raw with emotion. He took a step back and dropped his hands to his sides before fishing out his cell phone. "Maybe pictures will convince the sheriff to open an investigation."

The absence of Dillen was immediately felt as a frigid wind whipped her hair around. She hoped he was right.

They were about to find out.

DILLEN SQUARED HIS SHOULDERS. Going down a road where he told Liz his deepest fears or let her into places that hadn't seen the light in forever wasn't a good idea. So, he distracted himself by taking pictures of where Pop had been found.

Liz did the same.

"There are no work-boot imprints in this entire section," she finally said after dropping her cell into her handbag. Wind whipped her hair around, and her teeth chattered despite wearing a coat.

He needed to get her out of here before she froze. "I think we have enough to take to the sheriff."

"Okay," she said, taking a few steps toward the Honda. She paused when he didn't immediately follow. "Do you need a few minutes alone?"

"Do you mind?" he asked. As far as he was concerned, this was sacred ground. This was where his father had taken some of his last breaths on his own before being hooked up to a ventilator in the hospital.

"Not at all," she said.

He pulled out the keys and tossed it over to her. She caught it like a baseball. Was that part of the benefit of growing up with four brothers?

His mind drifted off topic, wishing he could think about anything else right now. As long as he was wishing, he might as well go all in and wish Pop was still alive. There was so much Dillen would say to his father now that he was a grown man.

A tear pushed through and fell onto his sherpa-lined denim coat. The thought of some bastard walking away and leaving Pop out here in the cold caused

Dillen's jaw to clench so tight he thought a tooth might crack.

Glancing around, he took note of how isolated this construction area was. Whoever was responsible for Pop's murder had wanted to make sure he hadn't been found right away.

This was a time when folks went home to see their families. Construction workers came in from all over Texas, Oklahoma and Louisiana to work on crews in these parts. There were never enough young locals for a project the scale of this one.

Had one of the men who worked here come across Pop? Had Pop put someone off without realizing he was being offensive? Being on the spectrum could come off different if someone didn't know what was really going on in his brain. He could be obstinate to the point of frustrating. Had he argued with someone over a parking spot? Someone who was angry enough to track Pop down?

Dillen shook his head. Didn't sound right. Who would become so upset with an older man who was on the autism spectrum they would murder him in cold blood? It didn't scan right. No, there had to be a reason someone would decide to end a life in this manner.

For one, this looked like an accident in the sheriff's point of view. Did someone go to great lengths to make it seem so? Dillen hadn't lived in Cider Creek in a long time. Was the sheriff lazy or incompetent? As an elected official, the spot had political implications. Folks were placed in certain positions because certain constituents needed law enforcement to look the other way. As much as he didn't believe Cider Creek was that kind of town, sheriff positions covered the county. Dillen couldn't speak for the rest of the county as to whether or not the law was above board.

Folks moved to rural places for all kinds of reasons, some of them bad. There were meth lab busts in the country as well as human-trafficking rings.

His thoughts were all over the place.

It occurred to him that his father might have stumbled upon something he shouldn't have. Being a witness could've gotten him in trouble. He might not have even realized what he'd seen, but a criminal wouldn't have known that. Pop might have been out in his old truck, and the bastards might have driven it home. A quick check of his wallet would've given away his address.

Now Dillen's mind was firing on more possibilities. Any of these reasons made more sense to him than Pop wandering onto a construction site during an ice storm and being pinned by debris.

Maybe Mr. Martin, who'd been at the hospital last night, would know something about Pop's comings and goings. Plus, where was his cell phone? Was it around the jobsite?

Using care, Dillen shifted a few pieces of Sheetrock around, searching for a cell phone. He didn't immediately find anything. Since he didn't want to disturb a possible crime scene more than he had to, he stood up, checked on Liz in the car and then headed her way.

The photos should've been enough to convince law enforcement to open a case. As he rejoined Liz in the car, the heater blasted him.

"What were you looking for?" she asked, cutting down the temp.

"Pop's cell phone," he said, pulling out his own and looking up directions to the sheriff's office.

"Why didn't you try to call it while we were out here?" she asked.

"The battery would long be dead by now." He propped his phone inside the drink holder.

"Did the hospital give you his personal effects?" she asked.

"Now that you mention it, no," he stated. "They didn't, and I didn't think to ask for them, either."

"You'll have to go back and give them instructions on what to do with…"

Her voice trailed off. This situation had her choked up.

"I'm sorry," she said again.

"You can stop apologizing," he offered. "There's no need. You weren't the one who did this."

"True. But I'm not helping much, either, and I can't shake the feeling the information is right there, like when a word is on the tip of your tongue but you just can't seem to find it," she said.

"Still not your fault," he said, reaching for her hand. "I don't blame you. In fact, the only reason Pop had a prayer at living is because of you. Without you, he would have died out here in the cold ground. He was still alive when he was taken to the hospital because of you. The doctor had a chance to save him, it just didn't go Pop's way at the end of the day."

He hoped like hell she took every word to heart because he meant them.

"No more saying *I'm sorry*," she said with commitment. Good.

Dillen smiled at her as he navigated onto the road toward the sheriff's office. She didn't deserve to be sorry. In his book, she was a hero. "You don't need to beat yourself up any longer. You did what you could."

"I just wish I could recall what happened," she said on an exhale. "But I'm sure it'll come back to me at some point."

He hoped the information came before it was too late to do anything about it. His time in Cider Creek was limited.

Now maybe the sheriff could answer the mounting questions.

Chapter Nine

As Dillen parked in a spot at the sheriff's office, Liz checked her cell phone. There were a couple of messages from the family, who were checking on her. She would respond to those later. It was a strange feeling to have a family again after cutting herself off from hers for so long. She couldn't help but wonder who Dillen had now that his father was gone.

What about when he returned to his military service? Who would he have to lean on then? She had a feeling men who worked in Special Forces didn't sit around and share their feelings. Of course, she might be surprised to find out what truly went on while the men were out on missions or back at the barracks, but she suspected there was a lot of lifting weights and sports involved. Dillen had the kind of chiseled body to support her theory.

Neither one of them had talked about having anyone special in their lives.

Could the two of them stay in touch? Would he allow her into his life? Even if it was just to check up on him every once in a while.

He came around the front of the Honda to open the door for her. She took the hand being offered, ignoring the frissons of electricity traveling through her fingers and up her arm. It provided more comfort than shock at this point now that she'd become accustomed to the sensations. Now it was more like warmth from a campfire on a cold night outdoors.

"How long do you have before you have to go back to work?" she asked as they walked toward the red-brick building.

"I'm on emergency leave. I can take long enough to deal with Pop's affairs," he said. "But I can't be gone forever."

Liz had no idea what that meant. She could only hope it would be enough time to convince him to let her stay in his life.

"It should be said that I have no beef against your mother, by the way," Dillen said. His statement came out of the blue. "She was always a sweet lady."

The admission caught her off guard. Liz was also beginning to realize how fortunate she was to have a family who cared about her and how unfair her actions might have been to her mother and granny. They hadn't deserved for her to turn her back on them.

There was so much trauma at the ranch. Between losing her father and then watching the pressure Duncan had put on the family to be perfect. She didn't understand why her mother had put up with him for all these years. To her thinking, her mother had been weak. Lately, she was beginning to believe her mother possessed a strength like no one else to be able to hold her head up high and keep fighting after losing the love of her life.

Liz might go to her grave never knowing the kind of romantic love her parents had experienced. It made her sad when she really thought about it. Not that she needed someone to complete her. She was a whole person as it was. Period. And yet she couldn't deny her heart was starting to ache at the idea of being fully loved by someone.

Those thoughts took a back seat the second Dillen opened the door to the sheriff's office. An older woman who sat behind a desk stood up to greet them, no doubt the clerical side of the office.

"May I help you?" the woman asked. She had a full head of gray hair cut short and teased up. She had on iron-pressed blue jeans and a white blouse with ribbons in front.

"We're looking for Sheriff Courtright," Dillen said as the woman smiled at him.

"My name is Eleanor," she said with a nod. "May I ask what this is about?"

Eleanor motioned toward a pair of chairs sitting across from her desk. Liz and Dillen walked the few steps over and took seats.

"I have evidence that will prove my father, William Bullard, was murdered," Dillen said, looking Eleanor straight in the eye.

Her lips compressed, forming a thin line. "I'm sorry to hear about your father, Mr. Bullard." She flashed eyes at him. "I'm assuming you share the same last name."

He nodded that he did.

"Okay, then," Eleanor said before her gaze shifted to Liz.

"Liz Hayes," she supplied.

"I know who you are," Eleanor said, wrinkling her nose like a skunk had just sprayed the room. "I just thought I might be seeing a ghost seeing as how you haven't seen fit to show your face around town."

Liz smiled awkwardly. Being called out for the fact she hadn't been home in far more than a decade didn't make her feel any better about her life choices. Dillen, on the other hand, reached for her hand and then squeezed. His reassurance worked. Her stress level dialed down several notches.

"Nope, it's me. In the flesh," she said with an equally awkward smile.

"Good to see you," Eleanor said in a condescending tone.

Since Liz had no idea who the woman was, she assumed this was one of Duncan's acquaintances. His reputation as a family man was all over town. He hadn't been. She would've thought people might have figured it by now considering every last one of his grandchildren had moved away at their earliest opportunity. People believed what they wanted. "Same."

Eleanor clasped her hands together and placed them on top of her desk. "May I see the evidence?"

"I'd rather discuss this with the sheriff personally," Dillen said.

"It's just that I usually brief the sheriff on what's

about to walk inside his office door," she continued. She was probably used to being the gatekeeper.

"Tell him Dillen Bullard is here to discuss his father's murder," he said without missing a beat.

Eleanor stood up with a curt smile. "I'll see if he's available."

"Much appreciated," Dillen said. His gaze could cut right through a person when he needed it to.

"Coffee is over there," she said, motioning toward a credenza with a machine and pods next to it. "Help yourself."

"Yes, ma'am," Dillen said in a tone of voice that was military stiff.

"I'll be right back," Eleanor said before disappearing behind a door she opened using an ID badge.

"Now I see what you're talking about," Dillen said out of the side of his mouth with disgust. "I thought you were being dramatic about being a Hayes before. Looks like I owe you an apology. You have no idea who that woman is, do you?"

"No, I do not," she said, appreciating his disdain for the situation.

"And this happens all the time?" he asked.

"It used to," she said. "I honestly thought it might die down now that we've been gone for so many years. So much for that idea."

"It's like being under a microscope," he said. "Who is she to look down her nose at you for making a decision to strike out on your own? It was a gutsy move that should be applauded, not condemned. How old did you say you were when you booked out of town?"

"Same age as you," she pointed out. There were a few other similarities between them that probably didn't need to be discussed while she was feeling an even stronger connection to the man.

"Eighteen," he said. "I enlisted the day after graduation."

"That's when I moved," she said. "And I did it with money I'd saved. I refused to ask anyone for a dime."

"You started a business that young?" he asked.

"No, I had to work odd jobs to make ends meet while saving up enough money to buy supplies. Then it took another couple of years to decide exactly what I wanted to do and become good at it. Overnight successes usually take years."

He chuckled, and the sound made her heart sing.

DILLEN KNEW HE could be bullheaded, but this might've taken the cake.

"Sticking with a dream can't be easy when the odds are stacked against you," he finally said, ready to acknowledge he'd made snap judgments back in high school. He should have known better than to hang on to old notions, but here they were and he was doing just that.

"I started small," she said. "That helped."

His respect for Liz Hayes was growing by the hour.

"Funny because my business didn't really take off until I got picked up by a major store and now it has gone bonkers," she said.

"Who is tending to the orders?" he asked.

"I finally hired a second-in-command and brought

in several temp workers to help handle things while I'm gone," she said. "I only planned to be away from work for a week or two."

"How many people did you say you brought on board?" he asked.

"One full-time person, who has been with me for a year now, and three temps to cover while I'm out," she said, holding up four fingers.

"Look at your hand," he instructed. "That's how many people it takes to replace you. That's incredible." He wanted to say *she* was incredible but stopped himself. He was, however, beginning to see her in a new light. And he felt pretty damn bad about casting her in the old one.

The door opened, and then Eleanor's head peeked out. "The sheriff will see you now."

Dillen stood and held his arm out for Liz to take the lead. She did, walking in front of him and toward the door. He reached over her head to grab the door and hold it open for her. When she turned and smiled, a bomb detonated inside his chest.

What could he say? She had the kind of smile that could start wars.

Three doors down the hallway, Eleanor stopped and held her arm out like she was urging them to go inside. "I'll be at my desk if anyone needs me."

"Thank you, Eleanor," Sheriff Courtright said as he stared at the screen on his desktop computer. He stood up, introduced himself and then shook each of their hands. "Eleanor said you have evidence that you'd like to bring to my attention."

Sheriff Courtright leaned over his desk, his knuckles balancing him on the oak. The man looked the part of small-town law enforcement. He was tall and slim, wore a Stetson and was in head-to-toe khaki-colored clothing.

Dillen fished out his cell phone and pulled up the proof. "Take a look at these from the construction site where my father was found." He pointed to the cowboy boots walking away from the scene.

"May I?" the sheriff asked, nodding toward the cell.

"Be my guest," Dillen stated, offering it. "We just came from the construction site."

"How do you know these boots don't belong to workers?" the sheriff asked as he flipped through the images. He seemed distracted and unimpressed, two things Dillen didn't want to see from the man.

"As you can see, there are work-boot imprints around the site, none of which lead to where my father was found," Dillen continued.

"I was sorry to hear of your father's passing," Courtright said warmly. There might've been sincerity in his tone, but he wasn't hearing the implication of what Dillen was hinting at.

Dillen also took note of the sheriff's word choice.

"Thank you," he said, figuring anger wouldn't do any good in this situation. To be fair, he couldn't think of a time when he'd been trying to sway someone's opinion intellectually and it had worked. When he was trying to get information out of someone on a mission was a different story. Then his anger was one of his biggest assets. The men in his unit hadn't nicknamed him Pit Bull for nothing. "If you take a look at the evidence here—"

"I understand your concerns and I sympathize, but what motive would anyone have for murdering your father?" Courtright asked. It was a fair question.

"That's something I would hope to uncover during an investigation," Dillen explained.

"What about these pictures and the fact that I have unexplained bruises?" Liz piped up. She dug around in her purse until she located her cell phone.

This was the first he heard about her bruises. The information caused more of his protective instincts to kick in where she was concerned.

"Can you show me these bruises?" Courtright asked.

Liz took off her coat and rolled up her sleeve. Around her left arm, bruises formed finger outlines as though someone had grabbed her and squeezed. "How do you explain this?"

"Could have been the EMTs," the sheriff said after a thoughtful pause.

"And what about this?" she asked with a little more frustration in her tone, exposing her hip to reveal a massive bruise.

"Again, you could have been dropped by an EMT on the scene," the sheriff said. "The driver who pulled up behind the car you left running at the red light called in a suspicious vehicle. It's how my deputy found you and Mr. Bullard."

"Which doesn't mean she didn't walk up on someone who knocked her out," Dillen added.

"True," Courtright said. "But there are other, easier explanations for the bruising and the vehicle. In my experience, the simple answer is usually the correct one." He handed back Liz's cell after glancing through the photos. "Plus, we need a reliable witness or motive in order to open a murder investigation."

"I hear what you're saying," Liz said, sounding more than a little annoyed. "My head injury and lack of memory doesn't qualify me as a witness despite what I know in my gut."

"There was a citizen in here the other day who said lightning struck his dairy cow and now it won't give any milk," Courtright said. "Claims his neighbor manufactured the lightning. Said his gut instinct told him the man was after his business."

Liz issued a sharp sigh, and Dillen didn't blame her. The implication would make any honest person want to throw a dart between someone's eyes.

"Are you calling me a liar?" she asked, locking gazes with Courtright.

"No," he defended. "But I am realistic."

Before Liz could snap at Courtright, he put a hand up to stop her.

"Apologies if I'm coming across the wrong way, Ms. Hayes," he said, softening his tone considerably. "The message that I'm honestly trying to convey is that the mind is a tricky piece of equipment. Even when folks believe theirs is functioning full force, mistakes can be made. Folks can lock onto an idea, and reality escapes them."

"I understand where you're coming from," Liz continued, pushing her agenda. "Believe me, I do. However, my brain is solid and I know these bruises didn't come from EMTs. But let's just say they did. What harm would it do to open an investigation into Mr. Bullard's death? He was an upstanding citizen of Cider Creek my entire life, and I suspect his, too. He deserves justice if there was wrongdoing. Can you explain how his vehicle is still at the trailer considering the construction site is too far to walk, especially in the kind of weather they had that night?"

"He might have caught a ride with someone," Courtright offered.

Dillen shook his head.

There were times to speak up and times to sit back and listen. This was time for the latter.

"I've heard good things about you," she continued as though she realized she was making headway. "You're fair, and you care about everyone in your jurisdiction."

Courtright gave a slight nod of approval.

"I fully believe with every fiber of my being that Mr. Bullard was murdered," she said. Hearing those words caused Dillen's muscles to tense. No matter how many times he heard them, the response would be the same. "You can find the person and bring them to justice before anyone else gets hurt. Because Mr. Bullard figured something out or was in the way of someone wanting to do harm to the community you've been sworn to protect. I'm sure of it."

"Even if I did open an investigation, I'd have no idea where to start," Courtright said on a resigned sounding sigh. "Boots at a crime scene don't exactly make for the kind of evidence that warrants opening a murder investigation." He looked straight into her eyes. "Your family has been through a lot. More than any family should have to endure." His gaze shifted to Dillen. "It's not easy losing a parent. I know firsthand."

"Then do something about it," Liz urged. "Don't let Mr. Bullard die in vain."

"What other proof do you have?" Courtright asked.

"It was TV night," Dillen supplied. "Pop never left home on TV night."

"Doesn't prove he was murdered." Courtright stabbed his fingers through his hair. "His mind could have been slipping for a long time. How often did you come home to visit?"

Dillen was ashamed to admit the last time he was home. "Not often."

"Then how do you know his mind was solid or his routine stayed the same?" Courtright asked.

"All I have is the knowledge Pop didn't alter his routine," Dillen said, hearing the defeat in his own voice.

"If you can bring me solid evidence, we can talk about opening up an investigation," Courtright said. "Right now, we have nothing to go on." He clamped his lips together like he was stopping himself from making another comment.

Dillen locked gazes, daring him to say what was on his mind.

Courtright relented. "Your father had been keeping to himself more than usual lately. A group from the church stopped by to visit him on Wednesday evening out of concern. Talk was that Mr. Bullard was losing his mind."

"He wouldn't have answered the door on Wednesday. Anyone who really knew him would know that. He had a lineup of shows that he binge watched every week." This couldn't be right. Dillen intended to prove his father was murdered. The prints might not have been proof enough for Courtright, but they screamed *murder* to Dillen.

"That's all well and good, but folks change their habits," Courtright continued. The man's mind was made up. Unless Dillen and Liz could present new evidence, this conversation would continue going around in circles. In the sheriff's mind, Liz wasn't a reliable witness and Pop had been losing his marbles.

"We'll be back," he said to Courtright before leading Liz out of the office, through the lobby and out the front door.

Dillen intended to deliver on the promise.

Chapter Ten

"Why is he being so stubborn?" Liz asked Dillen the second they were safely inside the Honda.

"Good question," Dillen said.

"You must be good at reading people," she continued. "Do you think he's dirty?"

"No," he said, navigating onto the roadway. "But I want to ask neighbors about Pop's recent behavior. I'd like to know if anyone new has been hanging around the trailer."

"Do you think they *would* know?" she asked.

"Folks in Cider Creek know each other's business," he said. "I highly doubt any of that has changed over the years."

"Good point," she said on a frustrated sigh. "I know your father was murdered. I have no doubt in my mind. After visiting the construction site, I'm even more sure than I was before. Something bad is in the air. I can feel it."

"I can, too," he said.

Liz reached over and touched his forearm. "There's

no way we're allowing a good man's murder to go unpunished."

"The sheriff will get on board as soon as we can offer proof," he said. "I got the sense he wished there was more he could do. Without a reason to change his mind, I can see his point that an investigation might be seen as a frivolous use of resources."

"You got all that from being in the room with him?" she asked.

"Last night, while you were sleeping, I pulled up an article that said the public wasn't thrilled with him," he admitted. "Folks have been in an uproar about how their tax dollars are being used since taxes were raised."

"He did seem awfully hesitant to step up without overwhelming evidence," she admitted.

"All he needs is a good reason, and we didn't supply one," he stated. "But we're on the right track and his mind is changeable."

"He thinks I'm reaching for evidence when I talk about my bruises," she said, wishing there was more she could do. "And then he dismissed anything I had to say that relied on my memory."

"It's to be expected, I guess," he said. "Shouldn't be that way, but I can see how folks might be swayed into thinking you can't remember anything or any of your memories might not be dependable."

"Is that what you think?" she asked a little more defensively than intended.

"No," he said. "I believe you saw Pop's hand coming out of that pile of broken Sheetrock."

His voice was more mechanical now, like he'd distanced himself from all emotion.

"Your father wouldn't have changed his habits, either," she continued.

"You and I seem to be the only two who believe that statement," he said as he headed back toward the trailer.

"At this point, I'm not sure how much help I am," she said, not wanting to leave but needing to go home for the family meeting that was on hold until she arrived since she was the last sibling to return, and then head back to work. She missed being so busy that her mind had no time to wander or think about things like how much she was going to miss Dillen.

"Go on," he said, gripping the steering wheel until his knuckles turned white.

"I came home for a reason," she started. "When I checked my phone earlier, I saw a long list of work emails. I can't run my business from here and I've already been gone seven days. Temps can't pick up the slack forever. And you said it yourself, I do the work of four people when I'm in the office. Orders are stacking up, and production can't slip. I can't afford to lose my business. And let's face it, I'm no closer to remembering what happened."

"Like it or not, you've picked up a shadow until you get your memories back," he said with the kind of finite tone that said it was useless to argue.

Except that he didn't get to decide who followed her around.

"As much as I respect that you need to get to the bottom of—"

"That wasn't a question," he said, interrupting her. "Wherever you go, I go."

"Until what?"

"The truth comes out," he stated. "Besides, you need me."

"What makes you say that?" Now, she really was interested in hearing his answer.

He loosened his grip enough to thump his thumb on the wheel. "You can't be certain you're out of danger."

"No one has tried anything so far," she pointed out.

"Because you've been with me," he said like everyone should've been on the same page.

She wasn't. Being with him caused her to want things she knew better than to want, and she'd only been around the man roughly twenty-four hours. Imagine how she would feel if she spent days or weeks alone with Dillen.

"That's a fair point, but it doesn't prove anything," she said.

"You have a shadow whether you like it or not," he insisted, clearly digging his heels in.

Liz crossed her arms over her chest. "I'm fairly certain there are stalking laws even in a small town like Cider Creek."

"They won't apply," he said.

"How so?"

She couldn't wait to hear his response.

"You want me beside you until you get your memory back," he said.

"Really? And I don't know this already because…?"

"You know as well as I do that whoever murdered my father is still out there," he said.

"They could be long gone by now," she stated. "It wouldn't do any good to stay in town anyway. Plus, it could be someone who worked the construction site and has already left Cider Creek. There's no progress being made on the site right now."

"You saw the boot prints."

"What if the sheriff is right?" she asked.

"You saw the boot prints."

"Doesn't mean we know what we're talking about," she said. "They aren't definitive proof that someone murdered your father."

"Why are you doing an about-face now?" he asked, agitation in his tone.

"Because what if we're wrong and we spend days together before we figure it out? I lose time with my business, not to mention the fact my family is waiting on me to get home," she said. "I'm just delaying the inevitable."

"It doesn't have to be," he said.

"Inevitable?" she asked, but it was a rhetorical question. "Yes, it does. Your life is overseas, but while you're here, you have to take care of your father's affairs.

"I have a family waiting on making a big announcement that I'm avoiding," she said. "Because I don't want to go home and face that house."

"Is that what you think you're doing? Avoiding responsibility?" he asked. "Because someone who leaves home at eighteen years old and ends up start-ing a successful business doesn't seem like the kind of person who runs from duty."

The fact he made good points only frustrated her more.

"Life is easy for a broke solider," she quipped, wishing she could reel those words back in the mo-ment they left her mouth. It was a jerk move on her part.

Liz tensed, waiting for the backlash.

DILLEN DIDN'T NORMALLY get caught up in emotions. Taking a calmer tact, he tried to focus on what she'd meant rather than what she'd said. It didn't take long.

"You don't have to be scared," he finally said, realizing comments like hers were coming from a place of fear.

"I'm not," she defended, rubbing her hands up and down her arms like there was a sudden chill in the air. Like he said…fear.

"You wouldn't be human if you weren't at least a little bit afraid," he soothed. She didn't need him griping at her. She needed a calm, steady voice. He could be that for her.

Her chin jutted out in defiance. "I'm good."

"I hope that's true," he said. "Because if anyone deserves to be, it's you."

Arms still folded across her chest, she turned to face the passenger window. Was she avoiding making eye contact? His focus had to be on the road except for the few times he was stopped at a red light, but he could feel the sudden chill in the air.

The rest of the ride was filled with silence. Her wheels were turning, he could almost hear them.

"Mind if we stop off at Rosa and Macy's house before we head home?" he asked since they had to drive right past the sisters' place.

"I guess it couldn't hurt," she said.

"We can swing home for lunch after," he said. "You have to be starving by now."

"I could eat," she said. Her answers were short, which wasn't a good sign.

He parked on the gravel road in front of the Brown sisters' double wide. They were both divorced now and had reclaimed their last name from before marriage. Neither had children, so the sisters had gotten a place together to live out their golden years.

Liz got out of the passenger side before he had a chance to come around and open the door for her. Another bad sign. They were racking up. He wasn't ready to give up just yet. She'd agreed to have lunch together. He could work on her then.

Before they hopped onto the wooden deck, the front door swung wide open. Rosa stood there in a flannel nightgown that covered her from neck to toe. Her hair was up in pink curlers, and she had on matching fuzzy slippers.

"Macy," Rosa shouted. "Come look at what the cat dragged in." She opened the screen door, letting her yippy dog loose to run around Dillen's ankles. "And he brought a Hayes girl with him."

Damn. Everyone really did know the family. He was seeing what a nuisance that could be, especially when she'd been away for fourteen years. Folks in Cider Creek had long memories. Maybe his investigation would benefit from it.

Rosa's gaze zeroed in on him. "How long has it been?"

"Too many years," he said with a smile meant to disarm the sixty-plus-year-old neighbor.

"Where are my manners?" she asked, throwing up her hands. "Come on in."

The little dog continued its yipping.

"Chauncy," Rosa chided. "Get in here."

Dillen stepped over the dog and led the way inside the double wide. Liz followed, reaching for his hand. He clasped their fingers together as they walked inside. The decor looked like a time warp from the seventies. There was wall-to-wall burnt-orange carpeting, Formica countertops with vinyl flooring in the kitchen and doilies on almost every other surface. The furniture looked handed down from a grandmother. It was ornate and didn't look comfortable to sit on, more like a place someone sat to sip tea. There was a sizable flat-screen on a hutch. The TV was on with the sound muted.

Macy stood at the kitchen sink, water running with her hands buried in soap. The two might've been three years apart in age, but they could pass for twins. The older sister, Macy, had on a flannel shirt and jeans with the same pink slippers as her sister. "Well, I'll be. You're a sight for sore eyes, Dillen Bullard."

She turned off the water, shook water off her hands and then finished the drying job with a hand towel.

"Good to see you, Ms. Macy," he said.

"And who is that behind you?" Macy walked over, squinting her eyes at Liz. "I recognize you. You're Duncan Hayes's granddaughter."

"Yes, ma'am," Liz said with a warm smile.

Macy exchanged glances with her sister before offering sincere condolences. "I was real sorry to hear about your dad's passing," she said to Dillen.

Rosa motioned toward the sitting area, so everyone claimed a spot. Dillen and Liz sat side by side on the sofa. She sat so close, their outer thighs touched, sending heat rocketing through him.

"We'd been worried about your dad," Macy said.

"Sister," Rosa warned.

"What?" she quickly said.

"We should mind our own business," Rosa warned. But why?

"Pop's death might not have been an accident," Dillen said, figuring he needed to lay his cards on the table. "If you two know something, I sure would appreciate an update."

Rosa gasped before covering her mouth. "I'm so sorry, Dillen. I really am. Your dad was the sweetest man and…"

She stopped herself as she became too choked up.

"If this wasn't an accident, my sister and I want to help," Macy clarified.

"Thank you," he said.

"Have you talked to his lady friend?" Macy asked.

"I would if I knew who she was," he stated. "Pop's phone is missing, so I can't look through it. There wasn't anything on his computer hinting at a relationship, but I guess folks don't exactly send emails anymore."

"The best way to describe her is..." Macy stopped herself.

"Be blunt," he said. "There's no need to mince words with me."

"She was blonde, for starters," Macy said.

"Big hair teased out and bleached," Rosa added.

Macy nodded agreement. "She was busty and wore her skirts a little too short."

"They were hiked up her backside," Rosa said. "You could see cheek if you looked hard enough."

"Not that we did," Macy said. "The blonde was hard to miss when she got out of her vehicle."

"What did she drive?" Dillen asked.

"A fire-engine-red Jetta," Rosa said.

"I'm guessing you didn't get a license plate," he said, figuring it was a Hail Mary question that needed to be asked anyway.

"No, we didn't," Macy said with a note of self-recrimination.

"I only asked on the off chance you did," he said. "You probably would only have noticed if the license plate was original or unique in some way."

She nodded. "There wasn't anything special except for the vehicle. But she didn't always drive here. That was only a couple of times, and she never stayed."

"He picked her up?" Dillen asked.

"We assumed so," Macy said. "But then we were trying not to be nosy neighbors." She exhaled like she'd been holding in a breath for two days. "It's just we always paid attention to your dad since he was... *special* to us. Once you left, he didn't have anybody, so we cooked for him and took over plates."

Dillen chuckled. "I'm guessing he didn't like that too much."

"Not until we got the routine down," Macy said. "Once we knew to make lasagna on Tuesdays, he started accepting the food."

"He was a stickler," he agreed.

"But a good person," Rosa chimed in.

"That he was," Dillen said, wishing he'd spent more time with Pop over the past few years. "I should have come home more. Then I would have known about the blonde and anything else going on in his life." He put his hand up to stop the ladies from letting him off the hook. "He liked to video chat on the first of every month, but there were times when I was deployed that he didn't hear from me for several months."

"You were a good son, Dillen. Don't let anyone tell you different," Macy scolded, wagging her finger at him.

Was he?

"Wouldn't a good son be here to protect his father?" Dillen asked as more guilt surfaced. Could the blonde lead to answers?

Chapter Eleven

Liz squeezed Dillen's hand in a show of support. Beating himself up wouldn't change the past. She needed to remind herself of the fact every day, or she would be the biggest hypocrite. She was still conflicted over whether or not to call it a day with the investigation. Curiosity had her wanting to follow through, but this could take days or weeks and she had a life to get back to.

The bigger issue was feeling like she was somehow letting down Mr. Bullard, who'd been the nicest, purest-hearted man in Cider Creek. He'd been different but never looked down on her for being a Hayes. In fact, he'd always had a kind smile on the occasions when she'd run into him at the store or gas station. He'd always said hello to her and never judged her. The gentle soul hadn't care one way or the other about her grandfather or his money, power or influence. It was rare to know someone so untainted by life. Being a single parent couldn't have been easy.

"Don't you dare blame yourself, Dillen Bullard,"

Macy warned. "Your father wouldn't have wanted you to do that."

Dillen issued a sharp sigh before slowly nodding.

"What about others?" he asked, redirecting the conversation back on track. "Did anyone else stop by that you knew of?"

Macy placed the flat of her palm on her thigh like she was needing to prop herself up as though life was almost too heavy to bear. She locked eyes with her sister. "I never saw anybody."

"Same," Rosa said before wrinkling her nose like she'd just walked into skunk spray. "Just the blonde, and she was all wrong for your dad."

Based on the description, the blonde didn't seem like someone Mr. Bullard would've dated. But what else would the wine be for? And what about the coffee? Had he bought more out of routine but stayed the night at his girlfriend's house so often his supply had built up?

"We would have been happy for your dad if the blonde hadn't been so out of place here," Macy said. "Maybe we should have checked on William more often. He might have gotten so lonely that he was willing to spend time with the first person who showed him attention."

"If I'm not allowed to beat myself up, neither are you," Dillen piped in.

"Well, that's certainly fair," Rosa said, giving her sister a disapproving look. "We all did our best. No one knew what was really going on, and it's none of our business who your dad dated. I'm just sorry he's gone."

"Has she been by in the past couple of days?" Liz finally asked. "The blonde?"

"Come to think of it, no," Macy said. "Not that I'm aware of anyway."

The red vehicle would have stood out.

Dillen stood, thanked the ladies for their time and then led the way outside. He opened the car door for Liz. She got in, and they drove the short way across the road to get to Mr. Bullard's trailer.

Once inside, Dillen walked straight to the fridge and started rummaging around for food.

"Don't you think it's strange the blonde hasn't been here in days?" she asked him as she poured two glasses of water and then set them on the table before taking a seat.

He stopped what he was doing. "Yes, I do."

Based on his non-shocked reaction, he'd already caught on.

"The reason might be that she knew he wasn't going to be home," she continued, checking for a reaction.

"I had the same thought," he said. "If I had Pop's cell phone, I could figure out the nature of their relationship quicker."

"You don't think it was romantic?" she asked.

"On Pop's part? Yes. On her part? I have questions." He shut the fridge door a little hard. "There's nothing inside here to eat unless you want another breakfast."

"Let me check," she said, joining him.

He stepped aside and let her have a look while he checked his phone.

"The diner is still in business," he said. "We could swing by there for lunch."

She hesitated only because being recognized as a Hayes was getting old. "Let me check the freezer."

"We could order online and swing by to pick it up if you don't want to go inside and sit down," he said with a raised eyebrow.

"How about these frozen pizzas?" she asked, motioning toward the boxes. "They look good to me, and they'll be faster."

"Okay," he said, but the question was still clearly on his mind.

"I'm tired of being treated like Duncan Hayes's granddaughter everywhere I go," she conceded. "It's nicer if we stay in. At least for me."

"Understood," he said, reaching around her to grab the pizza boxes.

"We can go out for dinner if you'd like," she offered.

"I'll pick up food," he said. "I've been watching the way people treat you, and I'm starting to understand why you left fourteen years ago."

"Folks have it worse," she said. "I shouldn't complain."

"Feeling isolated in your own hometown is a pretty good reason," he said as she checked the box and then preheated the oven.

He pulled out a round pizza pan after she took the box and opened it.

"We might as well take a seat while we wait," he said, motioning toward the table once the pizza was cooking.

Liz sat across the small table from him.

"The military saved my life," he started. "I had to get out of Cider Creek. My earliest memories in school are being teased about Pop. I was a scrawny runt back then and got my backside handed to me for sticking up for him."

"That didn't last long because by middle school you were the tallest kid in our grade," she said. Her heart went out to him for the bullying he'd experienced. Kids could be jerks to each other.

"I filled out by high school, but by then everyone had left me alone," he said. "I'd developed a hothead reputation, according to the school counselor."

"You had good reason after being bullied."

"I ended up with a chip on my shoulder that not even fourteen years in the military spent fighting a real enemy could fix," he continued. "If I'm honest, it's still there."

"Seems like you have it under control," she said. Although to be fair, he'd been hard on her recently.

"I'm trying," he said before taking a sip of water. "It's not always easy, though."

"Must have been difficult on your relationships," she said.

"What relationships?" he countered with a half-cocked smile.

"Come on, Dillen. A hot guy like you must have

been with plenty of women," she continued, half wanting to know the answer and half not.

"Not really," he said on a shrug. "I'm deployed a lot, so I'm fighting most of the time."

"What's the saying about soldiers? A girl in every port?"

"It's partially true," he said. "But not for me. There are people I see on a regular basis when I'm on base. They don't need to be in a relationship any more than I do."

"What makes you say that?"

She really was curious.

"What about you?" he asked, turning the tables at the moment the oven timer dinged.

"Saved by the bell," she said, hopping up to get the pizzas.

He joined her, opening a drawer and pulling out a pizza cutter. He cut slices, then she placed them on plates before he slid a second pizza in the oven. They made a good team in the kitchen.

What about in the bedroom?

Liz's cheeks flamed just thinking about the two of them in bed together. She needed to redirect her thoughts before she ended up down the rabbit hole.

DILLEN GRABBED BOTH plates and headed back to the table while the second pizza did its thing. "You were just about to tell me about your relationship status."

"Single," she said. The red flush to her cheeks made her even more beautiful if that was possible. "I was in a relationship that became suffocating."

"I'm guessing he wanted to spend twenty-four seven together," he said.

"Not that bad," she said. "But he did ask for space in my closet."

"What an awful request," he teased. "I thought women wanted to be asked those questions."

"What about the women you spend time with?" she quipped.

"You got me there," he said. "I shouldn't group everyone into the same category."

"There are women who want husbands and children," she said. "There's nothing wrong with those things. They just aren't for everyone."

"Amen," he said a little too enthusiastically.

Her gaze immediately popped up to meet his. "You don't ever want children?"

"I could do without them," he admitted, thinking it would take a special person to make him want to settle down. Someone intelligent and funny. Someone beautiful inside and out. Someone he wanted to spend all day in bed with on a Sunday morning.

Someone like Liz?

Dillen smirked. He must've been exhausted because he'd just thought of Liz Hayes as someone he could see himself locking down with in a real relationship.

"What's so funny?" she asked.

He realized she was studying him.

"Nothing," he said. "Tell me about this guy. Why did you break up with him?"

"Kevin gave me an ultimatum about work," she said.

"Why would anyone draw a line in the sand like that?" he asked. "Plus, why wouldn't he be damn proud of you? I know I would be if my lady was crushing a business."

"Apparently I wasn't spending enough time with him, and he thought I was in a bigger relationship with my business than I was with him," she said on a shrug. "Demanding that I choose between a guy and my livelihood wasn't the best play."

"Sounds like a losing proposition," Dillen confirmed. It was a mistake he would never make with someone like Liz. Her business was her independence. It had been hard fought, and she'd done an amazing job. Any man should've been proud to be by her side, not whine because she couldn't coddle him every five minutes. "I'm guessing he wasn't as driven as you are."

She shook her head. "He had a trust fund to back him up."

"So? You could have one, too," he defended.

"I mean, sure, I guess that's true," she said. "But why would I want Duncan Hayes's money? He would have held it over my head and ruled my life."

"I'm guessing your siblings felt the same way or they would have stuck around town," he said.

"We're all so independent. I can't imagine anyone being happy under Duncan's thumb," she said. "I'll never know how my mom put up with him for so many years."

"She had six mouths to feed after losing her husband," he said. "I'm one hundred percent certain she did it for you guys."

Liz compressed her lips into a frown.

"You're right," she said after a thoughtful pause. "And that's probably the real reason I've been determined not to let anyone in. I saw the hurt in her eyes when my father died. I witnessed how Duncan took over. And the spark in her just died for a long time."

"Losing someone you truly love can knock the wind out of you," he said. He and Liz weren't so different after all. Both kept everyone at arm's length as a survival tactic.

"What about your mom?" Liz asked, turning the tables. "Do you mind if I ask what happened to her?"

The timer dinged, so he took a break from the conversation and cut the second pizza. After filling their plates with round two, he sat down and contemplated whether or not he wanted to discuss his mother.

Why the hell not? They'd talked about a host of other subjects. He realized Liz was a good listener and he actually liked talking to her. He'd never really opened up about his past before. There was something special about Liz he couldn't quite put his finger on.

"My mother left after dropping me off to my first day of kindergarten," he began. A sharp pain in the center of his chest had him wondering if talking about his mother was a good idea. He didn't go there with anyone. Not even Pop had talked about her after that day. "She said all these things to me that my five-year-old brain thought was to comfort me to get through that day. But no, she had other plans."

"That's so unfair," Liz said with the kind of compassion that was balm to a wounded heart. "You didn't deserve to have that happen to you."

"I appreciate it," he said, getting choked up talking about the past. "But it's good to finally tell someone. It's like this has been bottled up inside me for so long that I've become used to living with the anger."

"What did your mother say, if you don't mind my asking?" she said, reaching across the table to touch his hand.

"That I should be brave," he said. Liz's touch had a soothing effect like he'd never experienced before. "That it didn't matter what else happened, I was going to be okay. I could handle whatever came my way. She'd said she was certain of it."

"You were five years old," she said, twisting up her face in disgust. "You needed a mother."

"Someone forgot to tell her that," he said. "The funny thing is she never said that it wasn't my fault. So, when she wasn't there to pick me up after school and the office had to call Pop, I blamed myself."

"It wasn't your fault," she said with the kind of conviction that said she believed every word. "You deserved so much more from her."

"Apparently five years was all she had in her as a mother," he said.

"Have you tried to locate her now?" she asked.

"Why would I?" he asked. "You don't have to tell

me twice that you don't want me in your life. Once is all it takes."

"No one could blame you for feeling that way," she said. "Even though you deserved so much more."

"Looking back, she must have realized Pop was on the spectrum," he said. "I always wondered if she was afraid that I was different, too. If that was the reason she didn't love me enough to stick around."

"That's a horrible burden for any child to carry alone," Liz said, standing up and moving around the table. She brought her hands up to cup his face while locking gazes. His heart practically exploded in his chest.

He stared into the most beautiful eyes he'd ever seen. The fact he could look into those eyes all day wasn't something he wanted to think about right now. All he really wanted to do was bury himself inside her and get lost.

His pulse thumped. His heart pounded. His breath quickened.

"I figured it out," he finally said, hearing the huskiness in his own voice.

"Sure," she said. "But that's a lot of trauma for a kid to handle. What did your dad say?"

"That's the funny part," he continued. "We never brought her up again."

"So you spent your entire childhood believing you did something to run your mother off," she stated. "Is that right?"

Denying it would do no good. So he didn't.

"The only thing I'd like to do right now is kiss you," he said. "But I won't do that unless you ask me to."

"Dillen Bullard," she started, leaning toward him, "I'd very much like for you to kiss me."

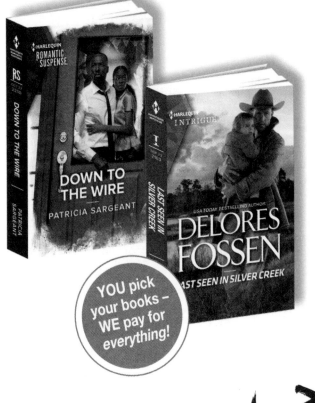

Dear Reader,

Your opinions are important to us. So if you'll participate in our fast and free "One Minute" Survey, YOU can pick up to four wonderful books that WE pay for when you try the Harlequin Reader Service!

As a leading publisher of women's fiction, we'd love to hear from you. That's why we promise to reward you for completing our survey.

IMPORTANT: Please complete the survey and return it. We'll send your Free Books and a Free Mystery Gift right away. And we pay for shipping and handling too! *We pay for EVERYTHING!*

Try **Harlequin® Romantic Suspense** and get 2 books featuring heart-racing page-turners with unexpected plot twists and irresistible chemistry that will keep you guessing to the very end.

Try **Harlequin Intrigue® Larger-Print** and get 2 books featuring action-packed stories that will keep you on the edge of your seat. Solve the crime and deliver justice at all costs.

Or TRY BOTH!

Thank you again for participating in our "One Minute" Survey. It really takes just a minute (or less) to complete the survey… and your free books and gift will be well worth it!

If you continue with your subscription, you can look forward to curated monthly shipments of brand-new books from your selected series, always at a discount off the cover price! Plus you can cancel any time. So don't miss out, return your One Minute Survey today to get your Free books.

Pam Powers

"One Minute" Survey

GET YOUR FREE BOOKS AND A FREE GIFT!

✓ Complete this Survey ✓ Return this survey

1 Do you try to find time to read every day?

☐ YES ☐ NO

2 Do you prefer stories with suspenseful storylines?

☐ YES ☐ NO

3 Do you enjoy having books delivered to your home?

☐ YES ☐ NO

4 Do you share your favorite books with friends?

☐ YES ☐ NO

YES! I have completed the above "One Minute" Survey. Please send me m Free Books and a Free Mystery Gift (worth over $20 retail). I understand that I am under no obligation to buy anything, as explained on the back of this card.

☐ **Harlequin®**
Romantic
Suspense
240/340 CTI G2AD

☐ **Harlequin**
Intrigue®
Larger-Print
199/399 CTI G2AD

☐ **BOTH**
240/340 & 199/399
CTI G2AE

FIRST NAME	LAST NAME

ADDRESS

APT.#	CITY

STATE/PROV.	ZIP/POSTAL CODE

EMAIL ☐ Please check this box if you would like to receive newsletters and promotional emails from Harlequin Enterprises ULC and its affiliates. You can unsubscribe anytime.

HI/HRS-1123-OM

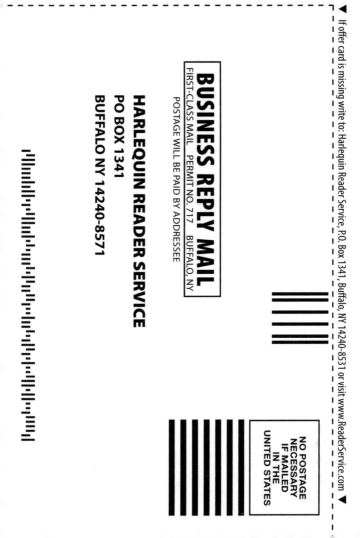

Chapter Twelve

Liz was used to asking for exactly what she wanted in every area of her life, except relationships. Until Dillen. Until now.

Placing his hands on her hips, his fingers dug into her sensitized skin as he pulled her on top of him. She straddled his thighs, all while locking gazes. Her heart had never pounded so hard against her rib cage. Her lips had never burned to kiss someone so much. Her body had never ached to feel someone moving inside her to this degree. To say she was stepping into foreign waters was an understatement.

Rather than run away from her feelings, she embraced them. There would be consequences, but she couldn't focus on those right now. All she could do was surrender to the tide washing over her and through her.

Dillen's lips were tender against hers at first, right up until his tongue slipped inside her mouth. Then his mouth covered hers with bruising need. Their breaths came out in gasps as she brought her hands up to his shoulders to anchor herself, digging her fingernails into his skin.

Her body hummed with need.

The air in the room crackled with electricity as he drove his tongue deeper. She bit down on his bottom lip, scraping her teeth across it as she released it. He groaned with pleasure, egging her on. Her full breasts were flush against a solid wall of muscle.

Tension between them escalated pretty damn fast. Another minute of this and she would definitely pass the point of no return.

Pulling on every ounce of willpower, Liz pushed off his shoulders and stood up. She shook her hands and paced a couple of laps around the small space, willing her pulse to return to normal.

She risked a glance at Dillen. The smirk on his face was a mile wide. He looked to be struggling about as much as she was.

"That can't happen again," she said, realizing kissing Dillen was dangerous territory.

"It probably shouldn't," he said, sounding less determined than she was to keep this relationship platonic. But then he was used to casual relationships. Liz might not go all in with the men she dated, but she gave as much as she could with her obligations. Running her business was her first priority. A man like Dillen could derail her focus.

Liz released a slow breath, trying to steady her racing pulse.

"You have to admit, that was a damn good kiss," he said, the corners of his mouth still upturned.

"No one's denying that," she said. "It's a good part of the reason it can't happen again." It would ruin her for other men, but she wasn't quite ready to own up to the fact to Dillen. He didn't need to know the full effect he was having on her body and soul.

It was most likely the circumstances surrounding them. Emotions were heightened overall, and they were both looking for some form of release. Sex with Dillen would do the trick. She had no doubt it would blow her mind. But that would make it worse when she walked out the door and returned to her normal life.

"We can't afford the distraction," she finally argued. No one, not even Dillen, could disagree with that.

"No," he said on a sharp exhale. "We probably can't."

Besides, sex would be a form of blowing off steam for both of them, and she wanted it to be more special with Dillen.

Did she just say she wanted to have sex with the man?

Her brain was playing tricks on her. She searched for a distraction. Her gaze landed on the table. Food. Right. Pizza. "Our meal is getting cold."

"So it is," he agreed with a long, slow nod.

A quick headshake later, and he repositioned to face the table, picked up a slice and chewed on it. His expression turned serious after clearing his throat.

"We need a way to find this blonde," he finally said. "I didn't see anything on Pop's computer."

"Now you know what to look for," she pointed out. "What about pictures from his phone? Mine sync up automatically with my computer."

"I'll check, but Pop hated being on the computer," he said. "I highly doubt he took selfies with a lady love, but it never hurts to investigate."

"Considering the fact that much of my sales are online, I don't know what I'd do without my technology," she admitted.

"I could do without most of it, honestly," he said. "I hate the thought of being glued to a device."

His line of work wasn't exactly tech friendly.

"I can imagine being out on a mission might make for bad internet connections," she said.

"I'd tell you, but then I'd have to kill you," he said with the kind of seriousness that made a shudder run through her.

Then his face broke into a wide smile. "Military joke."

She smiled back, making eye contact, which wasn't the best of ideas. As long as she kept a healthy distance from the man, she'd be fine. Being close to him was a different story.

Liz reclaimed her seat and finished off the last bites of pizza on her plate. After, she stood up and moved to the sink with her dish. Dillen joined her, standing beside her. She took a wide sidestep to put some distance between them. Being flooded with his spicy male scent was a bad idea while she was still feeling vulnerable to him. Give her a few more minutes, an hour, and she'd be good to go. Right now, though, it took an enormous amount of restraint not to lean into the man and pull from his strength.

Since he didn't seem as bothered, she figured the pull was much stronger for her. Her self-control needed to be on point from here on out. Besides, he would always see her as a Hayes, a princess.

"The past few days are really hitting. Do you mind if I wash up and take a nap?" she asked, suppressing a yawn. More caffeine wouldn't help in a time like this. Stepping away from the attraction with Dillen, she felt tired in her bones.

"Go ahead," he said. "The shower in the main bedroom is nicer. You might want to use that one."

She nodded, remembering she had suitcases in her trunk. "I totally forgot about having clothes and toiletries in my car."

"Where?" he asked. "I didn't see anything. Since you were going home, I figured you already had supplies waiting there."

"My trunk, but I'll—"

"Don't sweat it," he said, pulling out her key. "I'll just grab your stuff and be right back."

Part of her wondered if it was a good idea to bring everything inside. This was a temporary stop on her way home.

Before she could mount a protest, Dillen was heading for the front door. He returned as she finished loading the dishwasher and set the pair of suitcases down in the kitchen.

"I'll be in the office if you need anything," he said before turning toward the hallway.

She wasn't touching that statement with a ten-foot

pole. *Need* was a tricky word when it came to Dillen. Besides, she'd vowed not to need anyone a long time ago.

FOCUS WASN'T NORMALLY a problem for Dillen. Shifting his thoughts to more productive ones had been his lifeline on missions. So why did he keep circling back to the kisses he'd shared with Liz?

They'd been hot, came the quick response from a voice in the back of his mind. They had been—he couldn't deny it. What he couldn't understand was why they trumped all others. Liz was beautiful, there was no disputing that. And sexy as hell. There was a strong but vulnerable quality in her that drew him in. She could handle herself. And yet he wanted to step in and be her hero.

He needed to remind himself of the fact she was as close to royalty as one could be in these parts. Except after getting to know the real her, the word didn't ring true any longer.

Booting up the computer, he took a seat and rolled the chair closer to the monitor. What had he missed before?

After spending the next hour digging around, he realized this was probably a dead end. For one, Pop hadn't had an automatic picture sync, like Liz had mentioned. Secondly, Pop had rarely sent emails. His inbox, however, was full of ads for services like treatments for a larger sex organ and women who wanted to satisfy him.

Dillen blinked a couple of times at the brazenness in some of the scams.

Pop had had the internet along with a camera and microphone, which was how he'd taken calls from Dillen. The equipment was old but had gotten the job done. Dillen had been on Pop to upgrade for a few years now, but Pop could be stubborn when he'd really wanted to be.

His cell phone might provide better answers, but it was lost. Was there a way to recapture the data?

There had to be.

Dillen glanced at the clock. It was after hours on a Wednesday night. The call center for Pop's cell service was open twenty-four hours a day, seven days a week. Dillen grabbed his own cell and made the call.

"This is Jordan, how may I help you?" the perky male voice answered after he'd sat in the queue for a long wait for a representative.

"I'm trying to access cell phone data for my father's phone," Dillen explained.

"And what is the phone number on that account?" Jordan asked.

Dillen supplied the number and waited.

"Are you a primary account holder, sir?" Jordan asked.

"No, I'm not."

"Oh," he replied, sounding a little deflated. "I'm sorry. I won't be able to share any account information with anyone who isn't primary on the account."

Dillen muttered a curse underneath his breath. "Is there a supervisor I can talk to?"

"I'm afraid she will give you the same answer, sir," Jordan said. "Is there any chance you have a court order or power of attorney?"

How did Dillen say he hadn't expected his father to die?

"No," he stated.

"Then I'm afraid there isn't much I can do to help you," Jordan said. "Is your father available? I can give the information to him."

"No," Dillen repeated, not wanting to go into detail with Jordan about a suspected murder. "My father passed away unexpectedly."

"I'm sorry for your loss," Jordan said with compassion in his voice. "I really wish there was more I could do. Unless you have documentation and then I can direct you to our website, where you can make a formal request."

"It just happened, so it'll take a minute to get my ducks in a row. I appreciate you trying to help," Dillen said. The customer service rep had gone out of his way to be friendly.

"You're welcome," Jordan said, his voice returning to a level of perky Dillen would never achieve even if he tried. "It was my pleasure."

Dillen ended the call before smacking the flat of his palm on the desk. What else could he do to get the information? Calling back and pretending to be his father came to mind. Of course, he would need to have a lot of information on hand. They would most likely want a social security number, possibly an account password. That's where he came up empty. The other information was probably here in the metal filing cabinets. He would need to dig around and find it anyway now that Pop was gone.

A shot of caffeine would be nice about now. He'd been in the office for two hours hunting for a break. It was getting dark outside. Their late lunch probably qualified as dinner, but he wanted to have something in the house just in case Liz woke up hungry.

He had a hunch she wouldn't appreciate waking up to an empty trailer. She'd been through a lot in a short amount of time. Again, her loyalty to Pop came to mind. Sticking around when she'd easily could have left Pop alone in the hospital wasn't something a self-absorbed princess would do.

All his preconceived notions about Liz Hayes were breaking down when he looked at her actions.

Dillen put on a pot of coffee. There was something comforting about the smell of dark roast. Being here in the trailer made him feel closer to Pop. His heart clenched at the thought that his only family was gone, and his mind started spinning out when it came to taking the next steps. Would he sell the trailer? It seemed wrong since this was the only home he'd ever known. But why would he keep the place? Leave it here, empty, and who knew what would happen.

Rosa and Macy would keep an eye on the place. He could count on them to keep watch. But what practical reason could he have for staying put?

The sound of gravel crunching underneath boots out front caught his attention. Dillen moved to the living room window since the light was off. He leaned his back against the door and peeked outside.

The neighbor from the hospital walked up and tapped on the door. Dillen's gaze flew to Liz, who was asleep on the sofa. Thankfully, she didn't stir.

He moved to the door, opened it and stepped outside into the frigid evening air.

"You sure have grown up since last time I saw you," the familiar man said, sticking his hand out in between them. Dillen must have shot a look as he took the offering because the older man said, "Theodore Martin. You probably don't remember me, but my friends call me Teddy."

"Mr. Martin," Dillen said as he drew his hand back and stuffed both inside his jeans pockets. "I'm not sure if you've heard the news but Pop passed away."

"I'd heard," Mr. Martin said, his face twisting in sympathy. "Saw the lights on as I drove by and decided to swing by to offer my condolences to you and your family."

"Thank you for stopping by," Dillen said, not bothering to correct the man about the fact that he was single and his only family was gone. "Did you stop by the hospital?"

"Me? No," Mr. Martin said. "And, please, call me Teddy."

Dillen could have sworn he saw the man. Then again, Dillen could have been mistaken.

"I'm sure your head is spinning over all the decisions that need to be made, so I won't keep you,"

Teddy said. "If there's anything you need, I hope you'll call."

Dillen highly doubted Teddy Martin was a good friend of Pop's. So, he wondered if the nosy neighbor was here snooping around for a story. Folks could be like that in these parts. They sniffed out gossip and wanted to dig around for something to talk about over a beer.

He dismissed the older man as wanting news to feed the rumor mill.

"Your dad and I had been talking," Teddy said as his face twisted into a constipated expression. He put his hands on his hips like he was debating whether or not he should continue. "We signed some papers, but I don't want you worrying about that right now. We'll get it all figured out soon enough."

"What papers?" Dillen asked, concerned.

"It has to do with water rights," Teddy said, "but it can—"

"A big part of my job while I'm home is finalizing Pop's affairs," Dillen stated. "I can't do that if I don't know what we're talking about here."

"That's a good point, son." Teddy threw his hands in the air with dramatic flair.

"Is a lawyer involved?" Dillen asked.

"It was more like a handshake deal," Teddy continued. "There are papers but nothing on me." He dropped his hands to his waist. "I just wanted to put that on your radar. I'll drop off the document."

"What are they going to say?" Dillen pushed.

"Oh, just that we made a deal for me to use a little

bit of water supply on his property," Teddy explained. "Nothing to get too worked up about." Teddy put his hands up in the surrender position. "I bet you have a lot on your plate already."

"I'm just getting started but this sounds important," he said, figuring he was going to be buried in paperwork.

"Have arrangements been made, or are those still in the works?" Teddy asked. Dillen noticed the change in subject. "The wife would like us to pay our respects."

He issued a sharp sigh. "It's in the works."

"I'll leave you to it, then," Teddy said, "I didn't intend to take up this much of your time. I'm back there in case you need me."

His land was directly behind Pop's, where he had a small family-owned cattle ranch. The connection was coming back the more time Dillen spent with the neighbor.

"Will do," he said to Teddy before the man turned and walked away. Had he come all this way on foot?

Cold air cut right through Dillen's shirt, so he headed back inside, locking the door behind him. More of that anger surfaced—anger he needed to get a grip on because the last thing he should do was unleash it on a civilian.

A few deep breaths later, he turned around and leaned his back against the front door. Eyes closed, he tried to force a calm that he didn't feel. Feelings were the brain's tricks. Their hardwiring could be changed. He'd become an expert at compartmentalizing his when he needed to complete a mission.

"Hey," Liz said. The sound of her sleepy voice opened his eyes.

"Hey back," he said.

"I heard voices outside," she said, shifting the covers and sitting upright. She crossed her legs and wrapped the blanket around her shoulders.

"A neighbor stopped by," he said. "Teddy Martin. He lives behind us."

"Did he want something?" she asked, cocking her head to one side. The move shouldn't have been sexy on her, but it was. It wouldn't be on anyone else. There was something special about the way she moved.

"Just stopped by to offer his condolences," he supplied as he moved to the coffee machine.

"Ranching communities are good about taking care of their own," she said.

He nodded as he poured a cup. "Do you want coffee?"

"I'd take a cup if you're offering." Her sleepy voice tugged at his heartstrings.

There was something off about the exchange with Teddy. Dillen didn't like it.

Chapter Thirteen

There was something different about Dillen's voice. A distance to his tone now. He sounded deep in thought. Or just plain old tired.

"One cup of coffee," he said as he walked over and placed hers on the table in front of her.

"Thank you," she said, leaning forward to pick up the mug. She rolled it around in her hands, enjoying the warmth on her palms. "How long was I out?"

"A few hours," he said, taking a seat on the recliner. He sat with his torso pitched forward, elbows on his knees, as he held onto his coffee. In that moment, he resembled a man who'd suffered a great loss. All the hard casing normally surrounding him seemed to peel away, and he was just a son missing his father. Would it help ease some of the pain if they talked about him?

"What's your favorite memory growing up here with your dad?" she asked before taking a sip of fresh brew.

Dillen thought about it for a long moment in silence.

"Come on," she urged. "There has to be something."

He kept his head bowed as though in reverence to the memory.

"There is this one thing we used to do together," he started. "But it's just stupid guy stuff."

"I'd like to hear about it," she continued pressing. Keeping everything bottled up inside was a lot like holding a rocket in hand. A spark could light the fuse, blowing up everything within spitting distance.

"It's not that big a deal," he said. "When I was little, on the first night of summer break we used to go camping in the backyard. But I was afraid of the sound of crickets chirping, so Pop made up this story about the cricket king and how it was his job to save little boys like me. So, every time I heard the chirps, it was a signal to tell me the king was out making sure nothing bad could happen to me."

"That's the sweetest story I've ever heard," she said, surprised his father had offered so much comfort when it came to emotions.

Dillen shrugged like it was nothing, but his eyes told a different story when they locked onto hers and held. Their depths were like rivers with so much brimming underneath the surface. "We had a whole routine of going to a store after school to get batteries for our lanterns. I could pick out any kind of candy I wanted. It was usually something sour. And then we would make pizza once we got home. He always took that day off from work so he could pick me up from school."

"I'm sure you looked forward to it for weeks," she

said. "It probably made the end of the school year even more special."

"Pop kept up the tradition even when I outgrew it," Dillen said with shame in his voice. "I begged him to come inside, but he refused." His voice cracked, raw with emotion. "I was embarrassed by him. Can you believe that? What a jerk."

"No, you were a normal teenager," she said. "We all went through the same things."

"Yeah? Well, I'd give my right arm to have one more night underneath the stars with Pop," he said, standing up and turning his back to her as he walked into the kitchen and headed straight to the coffee pot to top off his cup.

Liz set hers down and then joined him in the kitchen. She put her hand up on his shoulder. He whirled around and caught her wrists so fast she didn't have time to blink. He immediately released them and took a step back.

"Piece of advice," he said, "don't sneak up on a soldier."

Dillen excused himself and walked straight out the front door. Liz knew in her heart of hearts that he wouldn't do anything to hurt her. But he looked angry with himself for his reaction.

She returned to the sofa and her still-warm coffee mug. Rolling it around in her palms brought on a wave of calm. A few deep breaths later, her heart rate returned to a reasonable level.

The front door opened and Dillen walked in. He closed and locked the door behind him before making a beeline to her. He took a knee on the opposite side of the coffee table. She was grateful to have a little distance between them.

"I'm sorry," he said to her with remorse in his eyes and more of that shame in his voice. "I came straight to the hospital from a war zone with no cooldown time in between, so I apologize for what just happened."

"Nothing did," she said, holding up her wrists. "Not even a thumb print. See?"

"It could have and that's not me," he continued. "It's not who I want to be."

"Okay," she said, still processing what just happened. "Surprising a Green Beret probably wasn't my best idea."

"It shouldn't matter," he said. "I should have had better control." He shook his head like he could shake off some of his frustration. "I'm sorry that happened." It was obvious how twisted up he was about what he'd done. Of course, he'd stopped himself from actually hurting her other than the equivalent of rug burns on her wrists from his tight grip.

"No more apologies, remember?" she said with a small smile. Dillen was far from an abusive person, so she wasn't worried about that. She was, however, concerned about his mental state. Was he in the right frame of mind to deal with the grief of losing his family?

Dillen dropped his head. "I would never forgive myself if I hurt you."

"You didn't," she soothed, remembering the tortured look in his eyes after he realized what he'd done. It must've been hell living inside his head. The man could have easily snapped her in two, but he hadn't. "You stopped yourself. *You* did that."

"Yeah, but what if I hadn't," he said low and under his breath.

"Wasn't an option, Dillen," she said, responding even if he hadn't intended for her to hear him. "You wouldn't have hurt me."

"How do you know?" he asked, briefly lifting his head enough to lock gazes for a few seconds. The uncertainty in his eyes was a knife stab to her chest.

She didn't have a solid reason to offer except to say, "You just wouldn't have done it."

"I'm glad you believe that," he said through clenched teeth, adding, "because I don't, and what just happened scares the hell out of me."

"That's just the thing," she countered. "Nothing *did* happen."

He just looked at her. "You have no idea what you just escaped, do you?"

"I'm right here," she said. "Alive. Fine. Unhurt."

"Your wrists might argue differently," he said.

She held them up. "They're a little red."

"I hurt you," he said.

Her wrists were nothing compared to the kind of hurt a man like Dillen could inflict on her heart. This wasn't the time to point it out, though.

"I'm fine," she argued. "Look at me."

He didn't seem able to make eye contact this time.

"ON SECOND THOUGHT, it might be best for you to head over to your family ranch tomorrow," Dillen said, still shocked at his own behavior. She was letting him off too easily because she had no idea what he was capable of. He did, which was exactly the reason she should go.

"What if I've changed my mind?" Liz asked, curling her legs up on the couch and then wrapping her arms around them. "What if I want to stick around?"

Her comment surprised him because he figured she would jump at the chance to be rid of him. Did he want her to go? No. Should he push her to leave? Hell yes.

"It's your call, Liz," he said as calmly as he could. She was clearly digging her heels in the more he fought her on this. The woman could be infuriatingly stubborn when she wanted to be. And even when she didn't. "I won't force you to go, but I think it's best if you do."

"You're giving me whiplash, Dillen," she said, studying him. "Earlier, you didn't want me to leave, and now you're practically forcing me to. I shouldn't have caught you off guard. I won't do it again. Problem solved."

If only she knew how dangerous a soldier coming in hot like him could be. She was right about one thing, though. He would cut his arm off before he would do anything to hurt her intentionally. It was the unintentional that had him concerned.

Liz patted the spot on the couch next to her. "Sit with me?"

He shouldn't. He should get up and walk into the bedroom and lock himself inside. But what did he do? He got up and took a seat next to her.

Why? Because she'd asked him to and he figured he owed her at least that much after what had happened. If she was willing to stay, he wasn't going to be the one to tell her not to. Not anymore. Besides, his willpower was fading when it came to her. The kisses they'd shared had been burned into his memory. Tension tightened his muscles just thinking about it. Sex…well hell, he couldn't even go there. Suffice it to say, it would be the best sex he'd ever experienced. Their connection was too deep for anything less.

But damn, fighting his own demons wasn't making life easier.

"Hey," she said.

He turned to look at her as she brought her fingers up to graze his jawline. She dropped her hand to his, and he linked their fingers.

Dillen had no idea how long they sat there, but it was the most peaceful he'd been in far too long. There was something basic and simple about sitting on the couch, almost like they were back in high school.

"What's on the agenda for tomorrow?" she finally asked, leaning her head on his shoulder while getting more comfortable.

"Should you stop by to see your family?" he asked, thinking they could work it in.

"That might be nice," she said. "Did you know Darren has twins?"

"With your sister?" he asked, not hiding his shock.

"No," she said with a smile that could light a cave on a cloudless day. "He was married before but lost his wife in an accident. I've seen pictures of his twins. They're adorable."

"Damn," he said, thinking he'd been so wrapped up in his own problems that he'd neglected his friend. "I haven't see or spoken to Darren in years."

"A lot has happened since the two of you talked then," she said. "But he and Reese are happy as larks, according to the family."

"Good for him," Dillen said. He couldn't imagine falling in love, getting married, starting a family and then losing the key figure in his life. And he felt like a crappy friend for not knowing any of this until now. "He deserves to be happy."

"They seem like a great couple," Liz said.

"Is he at the ranch? Does he live there?"

"Honestly, we can figure that out when we drop by tomorrow," she said. "I've been dreading this trip, putting it off, but it'll be nice to see everyone in person."

"It's easy to take family for granted," he said. "You think they're always going to be there, and then life makes a different decision and you just have to figure out a way to learn to roll with it."

She nodded, and he realized she of all people would understand. She'd lost her father at a young age. Was that the reason she'd kept to herself all those years?

"I might drop you off tomorrow so I can keep the

investigation going," he said, changing the subject. "After Teddy's visit, I'm also realizing that I need to make arrangements for Pop plus start taking care of his affairs—starting with what I'm going to do with this place."

"Have you given it any thought?" she asked, shifting to a more upright position. He liked the way she'd relaxed into him a few minutes ago. But this was probably better for both their sakes.

"Not really," he admitted. "Which is why I need to start."

"You could always talk it through with my family," she offered. "They're knowledgeable about Cider Creek and could probably give you the best advice as to whether to hold on or sell." She exhaled a slow breath as she looked around. "I'm not sure how you'd be able to get rid of this place, though."

"Don't tell me you like it here," he quipped, wishing he could reel those words back in. Too late.

"Because I'm a princess?" she retorted with indignation and hurt in her voice.

"No," he countered. "Because it's masculine. There's nothing soft about it."

"And...what? You picture me sitting in a purple room with nothing but fluffy pillows around?"

Liz leaned away from him now, propping herself up on a throw pillow.

"That didn't come out right," he said, reaching for her and tugging her over to him again. "This place is too simple and brown."

"It's calming here," she said after a few beats of

silence. "There's something warm and homey about the place." She shrugged. "And it reflects your father, who was a very good man who never treated me any different because of my last name."

Those words made it click in Dillen's brain as to why she had such an affinity for his father. It wasn't because she'd pitied Pop. Dillen could be a real jerk sometimes.

A loud boom shook the walls. An explosion?

Dillen hadn't expected to hear an all-too-familiar sound like that one back at home. What the hell had just happened?

Chapter Fourteen

Liz hopped to her feet at the same moment as Dillen. He bolted toward the front window, moving faster than a gazelle with a lion on its tail.

Dillen muttered a curse. "Rosa and Macy."

The bright orange glow shone brightly through the slats in the mini blinds.

"How bad is it?" she asked as she caught up to him.

"The worst," he said.

He was outside and gunning toward the massive blaze engulfing the double-wide in two shakes. Liz grabbed the blanket on her way out after feeling the blast of cold air from the door being opened. She threw it around her shoulders as she ran barefooted across the gravel.

Rocks cut into the bottoms of her feet. The wind slammed into her.

Where was rain when they needed it?

Another explosion knocked Dillen backward and off his feet as he neared their trailer. Nothing stopped him from getting right back up and running toward danger. He disappeared around the side of the double-wide, giving the fire engulfing it a wide berth.

Liz started to follow, then realized she didn't have her phone with her. She circled back to get it, praying Dillen would be okay. Her cell was sitting on the table next to her coffee. With trembling hands, she picked it up and managed to call 911.

"What's your emergency?" the dispatcher said after answering on the third ring.

"Fire at the neighbor's home after an explosion," Liz supplied, gasping for air from the run back, the cold and the stress. She glanced at the gas stove in the kitchen and then said a silent prayer for the sisters.

"What's the address, ma'am?" the dispatcher asked.

"Hold on," Liz said, needing to go check outside. There was nothing on the door, so she ran to the mailbox, ignoring the painful stabs to the bottom of her feet. She opened the metal box and retrieved a piece of mail. The flashlight app on her cell phone provided the light she needed to read the address. She rattled it off.

"And your name?" the dispatcher said.

"Liz Hayes," she supplied.

"And you said there is a fire following an explosion at your home?" the dispatcher asked.

"No, it's across the street at Rosa and Macy's home," she supplied, realizing she didn't know their last names.

"Please hold," the dispatcher said. After what seemed like an eternity, she returned to the call. "I have alerted the volunteer fire department. Please stay on the line while they arrive."

"Do you know how long it's going to take?" she asked.

"Fifteen minutes," the dispatcher supplied.

"The whole trailer will be gone by then," Liz stated. She couldn't stand here and do nothing. "I have to go."

Before the dispatcher could argue, Liz ended the call. There was no way she could stand idly by while watching Rosa and Macy go up in flames. She set her cell on top of the mailbox and bolted in the direction Dillen had gone a few moments ago.

Heart pounding, adrenaline kicked in. The rush had her pulse skyrocketing and her breath coming out in gasps. *Breathe.*

As she rounded the corner, she saw legs sprawled out. It wasn't immediately clear which sister they belonged to. The answer came a couple of seconds later as she neared. Macy's lifeless body lay there.

Liz choked back a scream, bringing her hand up to cover her mouth.

The back door slammed against the wall. Dillen appeared, walking backward, dragging a second lifeless body. Rosa. Her flannel nightgown was on fire.

Hopping onto the wood deck, Liz pulled the blanket from her shoulders and wrapped it around the small blaze. Then she helped get Rosa safely away from the burning trailer. Dillen's shirt was up over his nose and throat, but he was coughing the entire time. It was a scary, barky, dry-sounding cough.

"Go get fresh air," she said to him, shoving him away from the smoke.

Wind whipped it around, but it was clearly fueling the blaze.

Liz dropped down to her knees beside Rosa. The older woman's pupils were fixed and her chest didn't rise or fall. Liz dropped her head onto Rosa's chest and listened for any sign of a heartbeat. She got nothing.

Scooting over to Macy, Liz repeated the vitals check. Macy was gone, too.

Tears blurred Liz's vision as she placed her hands on top of one another on the center of Macy's chest and started pumping. It had been years since she'd taken a CPR class, so she pulled on the only information she remembered and pumped after clearing Macy's airway. Thirty chest compressions. Liz dropped her head down, placing her ear against Macy's heart. Nothing.

She pinched the woman's nose and then gave two breaths.

A few seconds later, Dillen was behind her, working on Rosa. Neither stopped until the thunder of footsteps filled the air.

Liz looked up and saw a pair of EMTs, one tall and thin while the other was short and stocky. Thin went to Dillen while Stocky came straight to her.

"How long have you been performing CPR?" Stocky asked as he took a knee beside her. He set his medical bag down and opened it while waiting for an answer.

"Almost since I called 911, so about fifteen minutes," she said.

"And how is the patient?" he asked, taking a read of her pulse.

"Not responding," she said as the first tear fell.

Liz wiped it away, tucking her chin to her chest.

"I got this now," Stocky said. "You did everything you could to help."

She was being gently dismissed. If anyone could save Macy, it would be Stocky. So, Liz stood up and took a walk to clear her mind and her lungs.

Within minutes, the place swarmed with firefighters and law enforcement personnel. Liz sat down, leaning against a tool shed, exhausted.

After what seemed like an eternity, but was probably less than half an hour, the blaze was out. Dillen walked over and sat next to her after being given oxygen by one of the EMTs. She'd overheard him refusing to get checked out at the hospital. At least the coughing had stopped.

Her nose and throat burned.

As she sat there, quiet, Dillen's hand found hers. There was something comforting about his touch.

Sheriff Courtright walked over to them and then crouched down to meet them as close to eye level as he could without sitting on the ground. "Are you okay?"

"Yes," Liz responded as Dillen nodded.

"What happened in there?" Dillen immediately asked, nodding toward the back of the trailer.

"The fire started from the gas being left on the stove," Courtright said.

"Neither of the sisters smoked to my knowledge," Dillen said. "I was inside and didn't see any signs of vaping, either."

Liz nodded as Dillen sat motionless, staring at a point over the sheriff's left shoulder.

"You're saying this wasn't an accident," Courtright said.

"I'm certain it was arson," Dillen said.

"How do you know?" Courtright asked.

"Turning on the stove doesn't lead to fire otherwise we'd all be dead." Dillen's lips formed a thin line like they did when he was angry and holding back a remark. "Someone lit a match or something like that. Plus, the glass on the kitchen door was broken. Someone came in from the back and turned on the gas stove."

"The glass might have been broken after the fact," Courtright pointed out as he studied Dillen.

"We visited Rosa and Macy earlier today," Dillen said, his voice scratchy. "They told us about a blonde woman who visited Pop. They were suspicious of the woman. And now they're both dead."

Liz bit down on a gasp. It was true. She suspected murder, too.

Courtright's gaze bounced from Dillen to her and back. "Is that right?"

"Yes," she managed to croak out with a cough.

Dillen pushed to standing, pulling her up along

with him. "I'm taking Liz across the street to Pop's house, Sheriff. I need to get her away from all this."

He held tight to her hand.

"You're welcome to come there for a statement, but she needs to change clothes to get away from the smoke smell," he said plain as the nose on his face. "We'll be there when you're ready for our statements." He started toward the house and then stopped. "But unless you want to treat this like a murder investigation, we don't have a whole lot to add other than the fact I ran in through the back and pulled each of the sisters out."

"I called 911," Liz added, but the sheriff would already know that.

Before Courtright could complain, Dillen had them leaving the scene. He was right. Unless Courtright wanted to take them seriously, there was no use wasting their breath.

"Hold on a minute," the sheriff ordered.

DILLEN KEPT RIGHT on walking. He'd said all he'd needed to and had no plans to waste his breath or his time if Courtright wasn't going to take him seriously about opening a murder investigation.

Liz tugged at his hand to veer over to the mailbox. She grabbed her cell phone from on top of it before walking inside Pop's home. "I'm glad I have a suitcase full of clothes with me."

"Take them off, and I'll throw in a load of wash," he said, pulling his shirt over his head. He stripped out of his jeans before he realized Liz was watching.

She turned her head away the second she got caught, mumbling something about going to shower and change before disappearing into the main bedroom.

Dillen took the opportunity to grab a shower, too. He grabbed his rucksack from beside the kitchen door and headed toward the bathroom.

Fifteen minutes later, Liz joined him in the kitchen holding out a ball of smoke-smelling clothes in hand. He took them and threw them into the wash with his own.

After pouring two fresh cups of coffee, he set them down on the table almost the moment a knock sounded at the door. After exchanging glances with Liz, he walked over and opened it.

"Sheriff," he managed to get out despite the frog in his throat. Dillen stood at the door, taking up the entire frame and blocking the sheriff's view.

Courtright's hands went up in the surrender position, palms facing Dillen. "I'm not making any promises, but I'm inclined to believe you and I'd like to hear more about what happened across the street."

Dillen studied the sheriff for a long moment. The muscles around his eyes pulled taut. Worry lines etched his forehead. He appeared sincere.

"Come inside," Dillen said, stepping back to make room.

"Thank you," Courtright said, following Dillen into the kitchen, where greetings were exchanged between the sheriff and Liz.

"Would you like a cup of coffee, Sheriff?" Dillen asked.

"No, thank you," Courtright said, joining Liz at the table, where all three sat down.

Dillen went first detailing what happened from his point of view. Liz recounted her side of the story, which was similar in the beginning to the point where he ran round the trailer and she retrieved her cell phone to call 911.

"Don't you think it's suspicious there was an explosion in Rosa and Macy's home following our visit?" Dillen asked.

"It's all circumstantial evidence," Courtright said, but his tone revealed he was just as skeptical as they were about the explosion being accidental. "If you're asking me as a person, I agree with you. As a law enforcement officer who can't act on intuition, I need proof."

"What about the fire marshal?" Dillen asked. "Will he investigate?"

"I put in a request before I came over here," Courtright admitted. "It'll be up to him whether or not he proceeds with an investigation."

"How do these things normally go?" Liz asked, her voice still as scratchy as Dillen's.

"The fire marshal usually goes with my requests," he explained. "Doesn't mean he will every time, especially since the last one didn't go my way. He might not want to commit the resources."

"Is there any way we can talk to him?" Liz asked.

"He'll get a copy of my report," Courtright said. "Your statement might make a difference."

Dillen noticed the sheriff didn't include him. "Because her last name is Hayes? Is that why the fire marshal will listen to her and not me?"

"I didn't mean to insinuate—"

"You didn't have to," Dillen interrupted. "The whole town cowers to the Hayes name. My family might not have the kind of money they do, but that doesn't mean we aren't trustworthy."

"It's been pointed out that you've been in trouble with the law in the past before you signed up for the military," Courtright said. "That doesn't bode well for me using you as a means to get folks to do things for me."

Dillen shouldn't have been surprised that once a label was placed on someone no matter how young, it stuck. The fact that he'd straightened up his act and had been serving his country for the past fourteen years should've counted for something. "As much as I'd love to be your 'selling point,' any logical person can see suspicious activity is going on here."

"I'm not disagreeing with you," Courtright said. "And I'd personally like to thank you for your service. You're doing this country proud. This town should be damn proud of you. But the Hayes name gets results. We don't have time to worry about whose word we use to convince folks to do the right thing."

Courtright was right. Still, it burned Dillen up.

He was more determined than ever to find the blonde woman with the red Jetta.

Chapter Fifteen

"I have enough to go on," Sheriff Courtright said as he stood. "I'll be in touch if I need anything else." He looked directly at Liz. "Will you be here if I need to speak to you again?"

Her cheeks flamed at the insinuation she and Dillen were a couple.

"I'll be around," she said. "You have my cell phone number if you need to reach me." She'd given it to him as part of her statement along with her address in Houston and information about her business.

On paper, she could admit to looking like a dependable witness. But so was Dillen. Just because he'd gotten into trouble years ago didn't mean folks should continue to look down on him.

Courtright nodded before letting himself out. She immediately got up and locked the door, realizing the threat was still out there. An ominous feeling settled over her at the thought. Was she safe? Had Dillen been right all along? Would the same person who'd blown up Macy and Rosa's trailer come after the two of them?

"Why Rosa and Macy?" she asked Dillen after a few more sips of coffee to relieve some of the dryness in her throat. "Why not come after us?"

"You heard the sheriff," he said. "It's all circumstantial evidence at this point. Rosa and Macy could potentially identify the blonde who'd been visiting Pop. We stopped over there to talk to them, which could mean someone is watching."

Liz involuntarily shivered.

"No one will hurt you on my watch," he promised.

Could he deliver? Even Dillen Bullard was human, capable of making mistakes despite being a highly trained soldier.

The determined look in his eyes said he wouldn't let harm come to her on purpose.

"We're going to have to watch each other's backs from now on," she said. "Three people are dead, and we still don't know why."

Dillen drained his coffee cup. "It's late. We should get ready for bed."

Despite the caffeine, she was so tired her bones ached. Even the nap earlier couldn't put a dent in her exhaustion. It was Dillen. He made her feel safe enough to finally rest after being in the hospital keeping watch over his father for five days straight. She'd scarcely slept the entire time except for grabbing an hour here and there.

"I need sleep," she said before excusing herself to go to the bathroom.

Her thoughts were spinning to the point that her head hurt. The headache between her eyes returned.

Sleep sounded like magic at this point. Had she eaten dinner? Could she choke anything down if she tried?

Probably not. The image of the sisters' lifeless bodies would stay stamped in her thoughts for a very long time.

Liz scrubbed her teeth. And then she threw on a soft T-shirt and sweatpants. Fuzzy socks finished off the outfit. Purple. Comfortable. She could use as many comforts as possible right now.

Her thoughts kept shifting back to the sisters, to Mr. Bullard's trembling hand and to the feeling they were missing something right under their noses.

She needed sleep to stop the hamster wheel of questions circling through her thoughts.

Dillen was sitting at the kitchen table with a stack of papers and his cell phone out while he studied the screen. She cleared her throat so as not to surprise him again. Liz was no match for his fast reflexes.

"Hey," he said as he looked up at her, his voice still gruff and his eyes red rimmed. "I just got off the phone with the morgue."

Liz walked over to the table and took a seat. "What did you decide to do?"

"Cremation," he said. "Pop left a copy of a will in the desk drawer, but he didn't have instructions for when the time came. I figure this is a way to bring him back here, where he was most at home."

She nodded before reaching out to touch his hand. The electrical current that came with contact felt reassuring to her now. "I bet he would like that very much."

"I need to decide what I'm going to do with this place now that he's gone," he said. "I let my unit leader know this was going to take longer than I thought."

"Does that mean you're staying for a while?" she asked, thinking she needed to deal with work now that he brought up the subject. She'd barely checked in since arriving in Cider Creek.

"Looks like it," he said. "Not more than a couple of weeks, unless…"

He didn't have to finish the sentence for her to realize he was talking about finding the person responsible and bringing them to justice. She could only hope that he would allow the law to do its job instead of meting out justice on his terms. She pitied the person on the receiving end of Dillen's wrath.

And yet she also realized how much he walked the line. Despite the sheriff not being cooperative at first, Dillen hadn't crossed any illegal lines. He obeyed the law down to speed limits and stop signs.

"Did you get approval to take the time?" she finally asked after getting lost in her own thoughts for a minute.

He nodded.

"Even without the investigation, I would need more time," he said. "I haven't even thought about what I'm going to do with his clothes, but there's no reason to keep them."

"You don't have to make those decisions all at once," she said. "Just start with the essential ones, and then figure out the small details. Besides, you might want to keep the clothes around for memories sake."

Maybe it was just that she'd been around too much death lately, but she was starting to wonder how much she was really living. Her business was thriving, and she was proud of herself for her accomplishments. Wouldn't they mean more if she had someone to share them with? Maybe Kevin had had a point. Maybe she was married to her work.

"We should try to sleep," he said. Dillen looked tired. He needed sleep. She couldn't imagine him trying to spend another night on the recliner. And to be honest, she didn't want to be alone right now.

"I just need to brush my teeth," he said.

"Mind if I curl up in bed in the main bedroom while you do?" she asked, putting her hand up to stop him from thinking she wanted more than to be close to him. "The thought of being alone with my thoughts isn't doing good things to my brain."

He nodded, looking like he understood more than he wanted to. "Do what you need to. You won't bother me."

Liz followed him into the bedroom and then curled up on top of his bed.

"Do you want your blanket?" he asked, standing at the bathroom door, looking better than anyone had a right to while standing there.

She shook her head. "I used it to…"

Recognition dawned. He nodded before half jogging into the living room. He returned a few moments later with the blanket he'd used.

"Thank you," she said, taking the offering and fanning the blanket out over her body. She was touched by the gesture and grateful for the warmth. She didn't want to climb underneath the covers on his father's bed, but she could curl up on top.

Dillen left the door cracked, another move she appreciated.

Liz closed her eyes. The image of the dead sisters stamped Liz's thoughts. She sat up and rubbed her eyes. Would she ever be able to shut them again?

BY THE TIME Dillen had finished in the bathroom, he expected Liz to be asleep. He was surprised to find her sitting up with the lights on.

"I can't close my eyes," she said as a tear rolled down her cheek.

He moved to the bed and sat down on the edge, thumbing the rogue tear away. "What is it?"

"The sisters," she said, twisting the edge of the blanket between her fingers. She shook her head as though trying to shake off the images. "I just keep seeing them. Macy with her blank look. Rosa as you were pulling her from the house." More tears fell.

Liz turned her face away from him. Was she embarrassed?

"Hey," he said in as soothing manner as possible. "It's okay not to be all right."

His training kicked in, and he compartmentalized the losses, focusing instead on finding the truth. But if he let those emotions bubble to the surface, he would feel just as awful.

"You don't have to be ashamed of crying," he said quietly, reaching for her chin and then slowly turning her to face him. "It just means you're alive, real."

She took in a deep breath.

"There's so much pent up back there—I'm afraid if I let it go, I won't stop," she admitted. Liz was the most real, most honest person he'd ever met.

"I'll be right here," he said. "I'm not going anywhere."

Liz pulled him all the way onto the bed, where he positioned himself beside her, backs against the headboard. She tugged his hand until his arm was around her, and then she burrowed into him.

He pressed a kiss to the top of her head before he could stop himself. She reacted by looking up at him with those big, beautiful eyes. It would be so easy to dip his head down and claim those pink lips, but she didn't need that from him right now. Right now, she needed to feel protected, safe.

So, he forced his gaze away from her beautiful face and just held on to her. He had no idea how much time had passed before she rolled onto her side and curled her body around his. Her steady, even breathing said she'd fallen asleep. Since he didn't want to disturb her, he grabbed a blanket to put over them. Then, he leaned his head to one side and fell asleep.

The sun didn't shine brightly the next morning. Instead, clouds covered the sky as Dillen opened his eyes and realized he'd slept until noon.

Liz was still curled around him, and he didn't

have it in him to move her when she looked so comfortable. Without his phone, he eased to sitting so he could at least run through the events in his mind.

"Hey," Liz said, stirring. Her sleepy voice tugged at his heartstrings.

"Good morning," he said, needing to put up more of a wall when it came to her. As it was, he was starting to lose grip on his emotions, which was not a good thing.

Dillen needed to put some physical distance between them. Besides, he couldn't remember the last time he'd slept a straight eight let alone more than twelve hours. But that was exactly what he'd done last night.

He pushed off the covers and slid out of bed.

"I'll throw on a pot of coffee," he said before heading into the bathroom to brush his teeth.

Liz followed, keeping her distance. She must have gotten the hint, and he hated the look of confusion in her eyes—confusion she tried to mask. If he didn't know her so well at this point, she would have gotten away with it, too.

Dillen sighed sharply before heading into the kitchen. He needed to refocus. A quick glance at the stack of papers he'd pulled, which included everything from the title to Pop's truck to his cable bill, did the trick. He put on a pot of coffee and then pulled out breakfast supplies.

Liz had to be as hungry as him.

She joined him as he started cracking eggs. "Move over. I can do that." There was a hint of hurt in her voice. She tried to cover that, too. Again, if she'd been talking to anyone else she might have gotten away with it. Not him. Not when he was so tuned into her that he could practically read her thoughts.

Dillen took a step back. "Mind if I take another look at the papers while you do your thing?"

"Not at all," she said. "I prefer it that way. You'll just be in my way if you stand here."

There was a sharp edge to her voice now that said she didn't appreciate the about-face. Damn. If life was different…if *he* was different, he might have something to offer a woman like Liz.

Sifting through the stack of papers, he remembered something Teddy had said yesterday. "Apparently Teddy and Pop had some kind of agreement. I looked all over the office while you were in the shower yesterday and couldn't find anything. That's when I came across the will."

"An agreement? Did he say what kind?" she half turned as the topic of conversation seemed to interest her.

Dillen shrugged. "Said this wasn't the time to bring it up, but he wanted me to know about it before I sold the property."

"Well, now I'm curious," she said. "Maybe we can swing by later and ask for a copy. There might be legal issues involved in selling the property if the two of them have a binding agreement in place."

Dillen didn't like the fact his father might've made a decision about the land or trailer without first consulting him. More evidence of him being a bad son.

It was mounting. He should have asked. He should
have known. He should have visited more.

Had Teddy taken advantage of Pop?

Chapter Sixteen

The afternoon zoomed by while Liz answered work emails and fielded questions. Dillen kept his face buried in paperwork, tearing apart his father's office while searching for additional documents he might need. His search wasn't fruitless. He came up with his dad's passwords in the form of a sheet of paper taped to the inside of one of the metal drawers.

Before she realized the time, her stomach growled to tell her it was past dinner. She pushed up to standing from the kitchen table and then walked down the hallway, making as much noise as possible so she didn't catch Dillen off guard again.

"Hey," she said as she stepped inside the office.

His back was to her, his gaze fixed on the computer screen. He swiveled around in the chair, and it was like the sun hitting her full force with its warmth on a spring afternoon. "Are you hungry?"

"You read my mind," she said. "We could do the diner" It might be good for them to get out of the trailer and talk to folks.

He wiped a hand over his face. "Sounds good. I've been staring at a screen far too long today."

Dillen stood up and then followed her into the living room, where they split up. She grabbed jeans and a sweater and then disappeared into the bedroom. After changing, she met Dillen in the kitchen. He'd done the same, having thrown on a sweater.

After slipping into shoes and putting on a coat, she followed him outside. He stopped on the front porch.

"I'm wondering if we should take Pop's truck," he said. "See if it throws anyone off to see it parked at the restaurant."

"Okay," she said, thinking it was a good idea. While he drove, she could scan reactions.

They moved to the truck and then drove to the diner. It was half past seven o'clock by the time they arrived. Business was slow, so there was plenty of open street parking.

Dillen had been quiet on the ride over. Was the reality of settling his father's affairs sinking in? Or was it being in his dad's vehicle again? Or both?

At least the fireworks show he'd been setting off inside when she'd woken up next to him had finally subsided. Dillen might've had it all, but he fell under the category of *complicated men*. She'd sworn those off years ago to pursue her business. Complicated men were distractions. Case in point, the way she felt about Dillen didn't match up with the short amount of time they'd spent together. Her heart had her wanting to go all in despite how much her brain protested.

Didn't real feelings take years to develop? Didn't real relationships unfold over time?

Dillen parked in an open spot as close to the front doors of the diner as possible. The gray truck was visible on the main drag, so they were covered there. He exited the vehicle first and then came around the front to open her door.

He immediately reached for her hand and then linked their fingers. She pulled back, releasing his hand.

"People will talk," she said by way of explanation, hating the hurt look in his eyes. "Everyone knows me. It's not like you can walk in there anonymously as long as I'm with you."

Dillen stopped and stood there, studying her. "I don't care what people say or don't say, and I sure as hell don't care what they think."

"It'll draw more attention, and you don't need that right now," she said, twisting her fingers together.

"You mean *you* don't need that right now," he said through clenched teeth.

She stopped herself from making an apology. "It's in the best interest of the investigation."

He opened his mouth to speak and then clamped it shut before holding his hand out to indicate she should lead the way.

Liz did but felt like a jerk. Did he think she didn't want to hold his hand in public because she thought she was too good for him? Because the assumption couldn't have been further from the truth. She bit back a curse. This wasn't the time, but she intended to clarify the misunderstanding the minute they were alone.

Dillen held the door open for her.

"Liz Hayes?" Georgina Baldwin came rushing over. What was she doing here? Liz had thought most of their classmates had moved to Austin, Houston or San Antonio after graduation. Some had gone off to colleges. Others had spread their wings and left the small town behind.

"Georgina," Liz said as she was brought into a hug.

Georgina's gaze bounced from Liz to Dillen and back. She smiled and her cheeks flushed with attraction. "I didn't realize the two of you were friends."

"What are you still doing in town?" Liz asked, distracting her former classmate.

"My parents bought this place a couple of years back," she said, tucking strands of her long brunette hair behind her ear. "I imagine they did it so I would come back home and help run it." She shrugged in dramatic fashion. "Guess it worked."

Her gaze zeroed in on Dillen.

"Sorry to hear about your daddy," she said.

He thanked her and then asked for a table in the corner.

"Sure thing," she said, recovering her bouncy personality after a moment of sincerity. "You can sit wherever you want."

Liz reached for Dillen's hand before she could stop herself and linked their fingers. He smirked.

Yes, she was jealous. Fine.

"Well, that was a distraction," she said after Georgina bounced back to get water, promising to return in a jiffy. "And who says 'jiffy' anymore?"

Dillen's smile widened.

"I just thought she might leave us alone faster if she thought we were a couple," she defended.

He put his hands in the air in the surrender position, palms out. "No skin off my nose. I would like to point out, however, that you were the one who dropped my hand outside."

"Good of you to point that out," she quipped, knowing full well what had just happened.

Georgina bounced back to the table with two waters in her hands. She set them down, and Liz couldn't help but notice how closely she stood to Dillen, especially when she bent over to set Liz's water down across the table.

The table wasn't *that* big.

"Are you back for good?" Georgina asked, directing the question at Liz.

"No," she said. "Just passing through for a family meeting."

"And what about you?" she asked Dillen. Could she bat her eyelashes a little harder?

Liz was getting snippy. She blamed it on stress and hunger.

"I'm out of here as soon as possible," he supplied.

"Oh, well then, point your phones right here for the menus," Georgina said, looking caught off guard at his curt response. His tone of voice had said he was ready to leave more than his words ever could. "I'll be right back to take your orders."

With that, Georgina disappeared back in the kitchen.

"She got out of here fast," Liz said with a self-satisfied grin. She retrieved her cell and aimed the camera at the QR code taped to the corner of the table.

"You're welcome," he said so low she almost didn't hear him.

Liz couldn't afford to get attached to Dillen, so someone flirting with him shouldn't have mattered one way or the other.

DILLEN PERUSED THE MENU, unable to hold back a smirk. He needed to wipe it off his face because Liz had been clear there would be nothing between them. She was right. He just kept forgetting the fact.

"What looks good?" she asked as she studied the screen on her phone. "I know I'm hungry, but it's hard to think about eating after what happened last night."

"You need to keep up your strength," he said.

She looked directly at him. "How do you do it?"

He shot a puzzled look.

"Do what you do and still sleep at night. Still eat?"

"You do what you can to shut it off so you can still function," he said.

"Sounds tiring," she admitted.

"It is" was all he said before dropping his gaze to the screen. "Fried chicken."

Liz nodded, but he could tell she was studying

him. No, it hadn't been easy in the beginning. After fourteen years of being a soldier, he'd learned how to shift his focus away from the things that gutted him. But were they still there?

Hell yes.

Was it the reason he kept everyone at a safe distance?

Hell yes.

Was it the only way he could do his job and keep going?

Hell yes.

The problem was that his usual coping mechanisms weren't working so well when it came to losing his father or containing his feelings for Liz.

"Fried chicken looks good," she finally said. "Definitely with mashed potatoes and gravy."

"I was thinking the same," he said.

"I should probably do a salad to pretend I've eaten healthy today," she continued as her gaze stayed steady on the screen.

He nodded. "Collard greens look good to me."

"Oh, those do look good," she agreed. "Okay. I'll have what you're having."

Georgina came back and took their orders. He remembered her from high school. She'd been one of the "popular" group who hadn't given him the time of day. Funny how things changed as he'd gotten older.

"Why not come after me directly?" Liz finally asked when Georgina disappeared for the second time. The corner where they sat was quiet. There was a dotting of four-top tables with a row of booths along the wall. And there was counter service to the right in retro diner furnishings. It didn't look like much had changed except ownership and some of the menu to add a few healthier options.

"We already talked about that," he said. "You've been with me."

"I've been with you for the past couple of days," she pointed out. "But I was in the hospital alone before that, and no one tried anything."

He shrugged his shoulders. "Could be there were too many witnesses around."

"I guess so."

"Harder to burn down an entire hospital," he reasoned.

"Sure," she agreed. "I see your point there."

"But you're not convinced those are the only reasons."

"Whoever is behind your father's murder went to great lengths to make it look like an accident on his part." She tapped her fingers on the table, a sure sign she was deep in thought. "Someone must have either circled back or was hiding, waiting until he…"

She shook her head like she could shake off the mental image.

"You know what I mean," she continued after a deep breath.

"The person might think you don't remember," he said. "Which doesn't mean you won't."

"I would think that would make me a liability in their eyes," she said.

"Maybe we're not dealing with memory loss with me because I really don't know what happened," she said. "The doctor said I hit the back of my head on flying debris or tripped and fell. I don't remember that, but it's possible someone came up from behind and struck me."

"What about the bruising?" he asked.

"The person might have gripped me to keep me from falling down," she said. "They may have been planning to set up an 'accident' for me, too."

Dillen took a minute to consider her points. She made a good argument.

"Plus, now, like you said before, it's too risky to come after me while I'm with you," she stated.

Georgina approached the table holding a server tray loaded with dinner plates and a breadbasket.

She managed to open a tray stand and then place the oversize tray that had been on her shoulder on top.

"Here you go," she said, placing Liz's plate down first and then Dillen's. The bread went in the center of the table. He took note of the fact that Georgina stood a little too close to him. So much so, she rubbed up against his outer arm when she moved. A quick glance at Liz said she noticed, too. He shouldn't have been happy about the fact even though he most definitely was.

What did he intend to do about it?

Chapter Seventeen

Liz did her best to ignore Georgina's flirting. It was a losing battle.

"Can I have a Coke?" she asked, figuring it would be a good reason to shoo the woman away from Dillen.

"Sure thing," Georgina said, whirling around and heading back the way she came.

The thought of someone lying in wait, ready and willing to hurt her—kill her?—wasn't doing good things to her mind.

Rather than go there, she picked up her fork and dug into her vegetables, giving the fried chicken a minute to cool down.

Georgina returned with the Coke, moving over to Liz's side of the table this time. She thanked her.

"If there's anything else you need, just let me know," Georgina said before adding, "It's good seeing you again. I hope you won't be a stranger while you're in town." The comments were directed at Liz, but she had a sneaky suspicion Dillen was the one Georgina hoped would come back. Alone?

"We will," Liz said, taking in a slow breath to

calm frazzled nerves. She was getting upset over someone flirting with a man who didn't belong to her in the first place.

The food hit the spot, and Liz was surprised she cleaned her entire plate. She must have needed to eat more than she'd realized. Of course, the pizza last night hadn't been enough to hold her over until dinner today.

She thought about the past, about Kevin. Life had come easy to him. All he'd had to do was step into his family's furniture business. Hell, he didn't even have to work all that hard since his sister worked there, too. Renee would cover for her brother in a heartbeat. In fact, she'd called Liz after the breakup and told her she would regret walking away from the relationship one day. Renee had reminded Liz how awful it would be to wake up fifty years old and alone with no one to share her life with.

Renee had accepted Liz into the family with open arms, so it probably stood to reason she would be upset with the breakup. Renee had taken it too far, giving Liz a hard time. Liz hadn't expected the two of them to be friends after the relationship ended, but she hadn't expected Renee to chew her out, either.

The fact that her ex couldn't stand up for himself and needed his sister to step in for him was another red flag and clear indication Liz had made the right call in walking away. Besides, he had too much free time. The man barely had to clock in any hours and was perfectly content to ride the family money. He was good looking and charming and could be fun. Liz had liked those aspects of him when they first started dating.

Being with him reminded her to take a day off once in a while and go out on his yacht on a Tuesday for no reason other than the fact the sun was shining. Ultimately, her need to be successful on her own and create something from scratch had driven a wedge between them. The fact that she couldn't go out every Saturday night, especially once her business had grown, had upset him more and more. His response had been to tell her to hire someone to handle "all that" so she could go out and play.

Liz just wasn't built that way. She was a Hayes through and through, a person who thrived when she was busy and took a great deal of pride in what she was accomplishing. He'd become jealous of her work, and she'd looked down on him for "coasting" on his family's funds.

The breaking point for her had been the yacht. The morning after the breakup, she'd had a change of heart and decided to join him on the yacht. Finding him passed out with Renee's best friend wrapped around him on deck had been the incentive she'd needed to walk away for good. They'd been clothed, albeit in swimsuits with barely enough material to cover, but it still had felt like a betrayal. He'd sworn nothing had happened "that time," but that wasn't even the point. The two of them had drifted apart, and she couldn't go back.

After him, she'd doubled down on her career, and suddenly two years had gone by without a relationship. She could admit that, lately, she was beginning to feel like it might be nice to have someone to share her accomplishments and life with.

She looked up from her reverie to find Dillen studying her. And then, out of the corner of her eye, she saw the widow Margaret Coker take one look at Dillen, perform a double take and then bolt in the opposite direction.

"I'll be right back." Liz got up from her seat and headed toward the door. By the time she managed to step onto the concrete sidewalk and locate the widow, Ms. Coker had managed to hop into the driver's seat of her sedan, start the engine and was already pulling out of her parking spot.

Weird.

Liz took note as she turned and walked back into the restaurant.

"What was that all about?" Dillen asked. The check sat on the table, so she grabbed her purse to chip in her portion of the bill.

He covered the paper slip with his hand. "Not in a million years. This one's on me."

Liz nodded and smiled. She could tell when she was going to lose a fight. She'd grab the next check to keep them on solid friendship footing.

"Do you remember the widow Margaret Coker?" she asked before finishing off the Coke she didn't especially want but felt obligated to drink now that she'd ordered it.

"I guess so," he said, his gaze shifting out the window. Recognition dawned. "Yes. I do remember her. Why?"

"Did you have a disagreement with her fourteen years ago when you last lived here or on one of your visits home?" she asked.

"No," he said. "Why would I?"

"You tell me," she said. "I'm only asking because she just took one look at you and bolted. I couldn't get outside fast enough to ask before she was in her car and pulling out of her parking spot."

"That's strange," he said, shaking his head and bringing his elbow up to rest on the table. "I haven't had any interactions with her in years. In fact, I don't remember doing anything that might have upset her back in the day. And that's the only time I would have offended anyone."

"There's no way she's connected to your father's…" Liz glanced up and saw Georgina heading toward them. She nodded, giving Dillen a heads-up that their former schoolmate was almost right behind him.

Dillen reached for his wallet, pulled out cash and set a few twenties on the receipt. "That should cover it. We don't need change."

The new information about Coker had his mind whirring—she could almost see the wheels turning.

It made no sense why the widow would be scared of running into him. Unless she had information. Or was hiding something.

DILLEN STOOD, ready to go. "Do you have any idea where Ms. Coker lives?"

"No," Liz said. "I don't have the first clue. Maybe someone in my family will know? Granny or my mom might be our best bet since they are the only two who stayed in Cider Creek with Duncan."

He nodded as his thoughts went down a dark path. How would Ms. Coker be involved in murder? It wasn't logical. She worked for the county.

"Let's head that way so we can ask," he said as he followed Liz outside.

In the truck, he glanced at the gas gauge as he started the engine. The damn thing floated, and they didn't have as much fuel as he'd first thought. "We should probably stop for gas while we're in town."

"Okay," Liz agreed. "There aren't any stations by the ranch, so it's now or never."

Dillen located a station on his cell phone and drove there. He got out and pumped gas. He realized Liz had picked up on the fact Pop had been on the autism spectrum. Looking back, he wondered if it was the reason his mother had walked out and never looked back. He had no plans to have kids, but if he did, he would be there for them every step of the way. The woman had turned her back on a husband and son. Was that part of the anger inside him that was always so readily available?

Opening up to Liz, talking about what happened was the first time he'd ever spoken to anyone about the past. The boulder that had been docked on his shoulders for what had seemed like his entire life was being chipped away the more he talked to her. Was that the reason he kept going when he normally pulled back?

He was beginning to realize the two of them had more in common than he'd ever thought. Both had been brought up by single parents. Both couldn't wait to get out of Cider Creek the second they'd been old enough. Both had a deep-seated need to prove to themselves and the world around them that they could succeed under any and all conditions.

Who would have thought?

Dillen's wisecracks about her bring a princess had grated on her nerves. Now that he'd seen a different side to her—the real side—he wished he could take those words back. He couldn't have been more off base about calling her a trust-fund baby.

He could admit to being wrong. His feelings for Liz had caught him off guard. The attraction had been instant and undeniable. And despite him being a complete jerk, she was still talking to him. That was something.

It was clear that she took a great deal of pride in all her accomplishments. Hell, she should be proud. Not many folks started a successful business, let alone kept one going.

Dillen walked inside to pay for his gas as another vehicle pulled up. He glanced back and saw there was an elderly woman at the wheel and no passengers. There was clearly no threat, so he kept going.

There was no line inside, but the attendant was busy in the stockroom.

"I'll be right with you," the young male voice called out.

So, he stood there, waiting.

A few minutes later, the attendant came jogging to the cash register, apologizing for keeping Dillen waiting. He paid with cash, which was his habit. He'd never like the idea of the government being able to track his every move when he used a credit card, despite working for one of its branches in the military.

Plus, he didn't like using plastic to pay for anything. It could get him into trouble if he wasn't careful.

A gas station attendant might notice if someone unusual came to town so Dillen decided to ask about the blonde. "Any chance a woman with platinum-blond hair who wore her miniskirts a little too short and drove a red car ever stopped by to fill up her tank?"

"Um, no," the male attendant said, looking like he was doing his best to recall the information. He shook his head. "I definitely would have noticed someone like that."

She would have stuck out in a town of blue jeans and ponytails.

It dawned on him someone wearing a ton of makeup and with platinum-blond hair might be covering up their real looks. Hiding?

"Thanks," he said to the attendant.

"No problem," the guy said before heading back toward the stockroom.

The bell rang on the door as Dillen walked outside. The sedan pulled away, and Liz stood at the gas pump with her arms folded across her chest. She was leaning against the truck and had a serious look on her face.

"What happened while I was inside?" he asked.

"I just called Ms. Coker," she supplied.

He shot a confused look.

"Got the number from my mom just now," Liz explained.

"What did she say?" he asked.

Liz moved around to the passenger side and reclaimed her seat. He did the same on the driver's side.

"I couldn't get her to talk," Liz said. "But she's holding back on something."

"Maybe we should stop by her house," he said, starting the engine.

"It might scare her even more," she said. "By now, the whole town must know about the sisters."

"I didn't think about how that might scare someone into going into hiding if they had information," he said, navigating back onto the roadway, heading to the one place he never believed he would be going… Hayes Ranch.

"She was off," Liz said. "I could feel it. But she swore nothing was wrong and that she suddenly remembered she had to run an errand when she saw us a little while ago."

"What are the odds?"

"Not high," she admitted. "No. She's hiding something, and I can't for the life of me figure out what it is."

At this point, someone had answers. They were close to finding them. He could feel it.

Chapter Eighteen

Liz didn't like the interaction with Ms. Coker one bit. It had left a sour taste in her mouth. With Dillen's background as a Green Beret, she had no doubt he could force the truth out of anyone. Ms. Coker was going to take a lot more finessing, which was something they didn't have time to do.

"Your silence makes me believe Ms. Coker doesn't like me," he said.

"Does she like anyone?" she asked. How did she tell him that the woman thought he was trouble? How did she tell him that the woman had warned Liz to stay far away from a man like him? How did she tell him that the woman had said a man like Dillen Bullard would only drag her down with him?

"Fair point," he conceded. "But my guess is that she especially doesn't like me."

"Said she was concerned about your type, whatever that means," she said. "Do you ever think that some people never leave high school?"

"It's part of the reason I got out of here as fast as I could," he stated. "Folks don't ever seem to change.

At least in the military, I meet different people. People who don't know squat about me or my background."

"Same here, except I moved to Houston," she agreed. "But I'm also thinking that maybe folks still treat us like we're the people we used to be because we haven't been around to show them any different."

Dillen stared out the front windshield like he did when he was contemplating a new idea but didn't respond. Liz refocused since they were getting close to the ranch.

Facing down the ranch with him gone shouldn't have affected her as much as it was. "How many of my family members do you know personally?"

"I haven't held a conversation that lasted longer than two minutes with anyone in your family but you," he admitted. "And that's only recently."

This family could be intimidating based on size alone. Six kids, with four of them being boys, was a lot.

As they pulled onto the gated ranch drive, he stopped at the security booth. The main house wasn't visible from the street. It was large, though, with eight bedrooms along with a guest suite on the first floor.

"Liz Hayes is home," Dillen said to the attendant as the man stepped outside.

"ID, please," he said.

Liz was already on the phone with her mother. She handed over the cell.

The security guard nodded a couple of times and said a few *yes, ma'am*s into the phone before handing it back.

"All clear," he said before tapping a button that opened the gate to the long drive.

Dillen parked before exiting the truck first. He came around the front of the vehicle to open her door. There was something comforting about this routine. Chivalry was ingrained in Texas folks, but their routine brought a sense of calm over her.

"I've been thinking about what you said on the ride over," he said after opening her door.

She shot him a questioning look. She'd said a lot and didn't know what he was referring to.

"About how folks can't change their opinion of someone if all they knew of them was the past," he stated. "I realized it's true because I expected everyone to still be eighteen years old, like when I last left. I've been back and forth a few times but never saw anyone from our year. I was shocked at how fast some folks had aged, like our old history teacher in tenth grade."

"Ah, Mr. Swinson," she recalled. "I haven't seen him recently, either."

"You might not recognize him if you did," Dillen said. "He has a full head of gray hair now and looks like he's aged twenty years."

"See what I mean," she said. "Our minds get fixed on our last memory of a person. If there's no new information to counter it, we stick to the same old ideas."

He nodded before placing his hand on the small of her back and walking beside her to the back door.

"Are you ready for this?" she asked him, but the same question could be asked of her.

"Ready if you are," he said after taking in a deep breath.

Their gazes locked, and then he broke into a wide smile. "You're going to do fine."

"Yeah?" she said. "So are you."

He pretended to slick his hair back and straighten his make-believe collar. "We got this."

The gesture was sweet and counter to his tough-guy image. Liz appreciated his sense of humor. Given the circumstances, it hadn't come out much. It would have been nice to have met up again under different conditions. Would they have spoken to each other? Or would those old opinions of each other have gotten in the way?

Liz opened the back door and walked into the kitchen of the main house. A hundred-pound Akita mix came bolting toward them along with an unfamiliar person trailing behind.

"Atlas, sit," came the command. Surprisingly, the dog obeyed. The unfamiliar face was framed by long straight dark brown hair with caramel highlights and bangs. "I'm Payton, your brother Callum's wife." She smiled a warm smile. "This is Atlas. Based on all the pictures I've seen, you must be Liz." Payton's gaze bounced from Liz to Dillen.

"Dillen Bullard," he said, taking a step forward with an outstretched hand.

Atlas growled from deep and low in his throat.

"Sorry—he's a work in progress when it comes to trusting men," Payton explained. "Best to keep a distance."

"Nice to meet you," Liz said to Payton as her older brother Callum joined them. He had dark hair that was not quite brown and hinted at their Scottish-Irish heritage with natural reddish-blond highlights. He was forty-two but didn't look at day over thirty-five.

Liz broke into a wide smile at the sight of her brother. "Wow, I've missed seeing your face outside of a hospital lobby."

"Right back atcha, kid. Got your text saying you were coming, so I let a few people know," Callum said before studying Dillen.

"You remember Dillen Bullard," Liz said.

"Right, of course, how could I forget?" Callum said, recognition dawned as he connected the dots this was Mr. Bullard's son. "I'm sincerely sorry for your loss. Your father was a good man."

"Thank you," Dillen said, shaking Callum's extended hand. "It means a lot to hear you say that."

Callum's gaze bounced back to Liz and the bandage on her head. "How's the healing? Getting better?"

"So far, so good," she said. "I have to go back to the doctor in a few days but I'm doing okay."

"That's good to hear," Callum said, some of the tension eased in the muscles in his forehead. "We need you around here."

Callum fired off a text, and then siblings started filing in.

"You know Darren and his twins, right?" Callum said to Dillen as activity in the room spiked.

"Darren, yes," Dillen said. "Not the twins, though.

I've been overseas for a long time and am afraid I'm not up to speed on life in Cider Creek."

"Don't worry," Callum said, blowing it off like it was nothing. "You'll catch up quick. Not a whole lot of new stuff goes on around here. But that's probably why you left in the first place."

Dillen grinned, and it was about the sexiest thing Liz had seen all day.

Rory filed in next with a girl who looked to be entering her teen years and was undeniably a Hayes.

"You must be Livia," Liz said to the niece she'd never met. "I'm your aunt."

"Dad has shown me, like, a ton of pictures of you guys," Livia said. "I recognized you right away."

Tiernan and Sean came strolling in next, phones in hand. A redhead introduced as Raelynn followed Sean, and another with long russet hair came in behind Liz's other brother. She must've been Melody.

A female with long blond hair walked over to stand beside Rory. She must've been Emerson.

"Where's Reese?" Liz asked after introductions were made.

"Around here somewhere," Callum said. He'd stepped into the role of taking care of the younger kids after their father had died. Liz had been young, but she still had memories of their father. Being here, seeing family pictures sprinkled around made her feel like she'd come home.

She reached for Dillen's hand, and he linked their fingers. To her family's credit, no one so much as raised an eyebrow.

After condolences were doled out and Liz explained the bandage and that she would be fine what felt like a dozen times, everyone settled around the oversize dining table. And then Granny walked in. Eyes wide, mouth agape, she couldn't get to Liz fast enough. She met Granny halfway across the room and was pulled into the kind of embrace Liz had been missing for fourteen years.

Granny tilted her head back and just looked at Liz as though taking her in for the first time. "You're grown."

"Yes, ma'am," Liz said.

"But I hope you haven't changed too much," Granny said with a wink.

"I wouldn't dare," Liz stated with that Hayes pride that caused her chest to puff up a little.

Granny was followed by a sight for sore eyes… Liz's mother.

"Mom," Liz said, turning toward her mother as she entered the room from the back door.

"I came as soon as I heard you were here," Marla Hayes said. She was five-feet-two-inches of kind eyes and warmth.

The two embraced as Granny turned her attention toward Dillen. Reese filed in next with a toddler on each hip. Liz never thought she'd see the day her sister looked like a natural mother, but the proof was standing right in front of her.

"I must be seeing things because I know Dillen Bullard isn't here in front of—"

"It's Pit Bull now," Dillen said to Darren as his

former high school friend entered on the heels of Reese and the babies.

"Damn, you look the same," Darren said before giving his friend a bear hug.

"Yeah? You look a helluva lot older," Dillen teased. "What are you? Fifty?"

Darren belly-laughed before introducing his family, his pride evident in his eyes. Could Liz ever change her mind about kids?

She would consider it with someone like Dillen.

DILLEN DESERVED TO be called a hypocrite and a jerk for the assumptions he'd made about the Hayes family.

There was another news flash—being around Liz's big family was nice. The jokes, the laughter, the love the Hayes siblings obviously shared for each was beyond anything he'd ever experienced in his thirty-two years.

"We came here to ask a few questions about Ms. Coker," Liz started.

"Can it wait a few more minutes?" Marla Hayes asked. "We've all been waiting a long time to be together under one roof and I'd like to make the announcement you've all been waiting for."

Deacon, the ranch foreman quietly slipped inside the kitchen.

Liz nodded. Everyone returned to their seat at the table. Even the children quieted down.

"As you all know, your grandfather is gone," Marla started. "So, I thought about what to do with the ranch and the land, but it seemed wrong to walk away from the one good thing Duncan built. Then there was all that vandalism going on, which seems to have stopped now that many of you have moved home or are in process."

Did Liz ever think about moving back to the ranch now that many of her siblings were doing the same?

"When everyone is together, we're a strong bunch," Marla continued. "However, I don't want the responsibility of running this place on my own, but someone in this room does."

Gazes shifted all around, searching each other's faces. Right up until the ranch foreman Deacon stepped up to the island. Heads nodded and smiles abounded.

"Deacon has been the glue holding this place together for a long time, even when your grandfather was alive," Marla continued. "It only seems right to hand over the reins."

"I couldn't agree more," Callum said. "My only concern is this is your home. Where would you and Granny go if not here?"

Deacon shook his head and put his hand in the air. "I have no rights to the family home. This is Ms. Marla's home, and I would never dream of taking that away from her or anyone in the family."

"Which is why Deacon will work the cattle and own the land beyond this backyard," Marla said. "We'll share the barn and pitch in whenever Deacon needs us or as all of your schedules allow."

"I don't need much space," Deacon added. "I'm plenty happy in the bunkhouse with my guys." He took a few seconds to look each Hayes sibling in the eye. "But I won't take the deal if any one of you is against it."

Callum looked at each sibling individually, no doubt looking for a nod or head shake. The nods were unanimous. "Everyone here thinks it's a great idea."

Deacon put his hands together in prayer position. "This means the world to me. This land and the cattle mean everything." The older man wiped at a tear that broke loose, running down his cheek. "I consider every last one of you my family."

"You've always been one of us," Callum said. Those words shouldn't have choked Dillen up like they did. "You deserve this."

Deacon saluted before excusing himself. He was clearly uncomfortable in the main house.

"Granny and I will keep this house, and it'll be handed down to you guys once we're no longer here," Marla continued.

Dillen coughed to clear the sudden frog in his throat.

"Now that many of you are married, engaged and have children, it's my hope that you'll consider coming back home for big family Christmases," Marla said. The comment got heads nodding and put big smiles on faces.

"A few of us were going to suggest the same thing," Callum said, glancing over at Liz. "You were missed this past holiday."

"You brought a dinner plate to the hospital for me," she said with a smile before asking if he'd seen a blonde driving around in a red Jetta.

Callum shook his head.

Dillen felt like a jerk for making all those assumptions about the family in high school and then holding on to them.

He looked at Liz and, much to his surprise, a real future sprang to mind.

Dillen mentally shook it off. He was getting caught up in the moment, in the idea of family. He didn't deserve one of his own.

Chapter Nineteen

"I have one more announcement to make."

Liz's thoughts still reeled from the first one her mother had made. She couldn't imagine what a second one might be. Although she couldn't be happier for Deacon. He deserved the world after all his years here, looking after the cattle and the kids while she and her siblings had been growing up.

"I've sold mineral rights to a trustworthy investor who will ensure no one ever does anything to harm this place again," her mother said. "I know each of you is self-made, and I couldn't be prouder of you for it. Your father, if he was here, would be bursting with pride the way each and every one of you have turned out as people." Her mom got choked up, and there wasn't a dry eye in the room.

Her mother recovered with one of her warm smiles, the kind that radiated from across the room. Mineral rights on the kind of acreage the Hayes family owned would be worth a fortune. The only thing that came close in value to a rancher was water rights. Those could be sold or leased for big money.

"You can do what you want with the money, but it's far too much for me or Granny to spend on our own, so we've decided to spit it eight ways to get the number down to something more manageable per person," her mother continued.

Liz really was curious where this was going, not that she cared about more zeroes in a bank account. It occurred to her that she could do a lot of good in the community with more funds.

"The number will hit your bank accounts today, but it's well into eight figures," her mother said. "Donate it. Keep it. Let it grow. Build a monument. Feed the hungry. I don't care what you decide to do with the money as long as you keep it in perspective, which doesn't seem like a problem for any one of you guys."

"I'm already doing what I love," Callum said. "So, there's no reason to rush into spending anything for me. But I'd like to start a family charity so we can pull some of it together and help the community."

"We sorely need a new recreation center with a decent basketball hoop," Sean chimed in.

"We can start there and figure out the rest as we go," Callum said. "As long as everyone agrees and feels good about what's happening."

"I don't have a problem with it," Reese said. "I can already think of half of dozen ways to use some of the money to help single parents."

Heads nodded.

Liz was proud of her family for putting others first. The stubborn trait from Duncan Hayes would pay off in the end. They would all dig their heels in when it came to making sure something good came out of all the money their grandfather had made. Something that made Cider Creek a better place to live.

She instinctively reached for Dillen's hand. He didn't move out of the way or link their fingers. But his muscles tensed. Was he pulling away? Why?

"Who can stay for coffee?" her mother asked.

Easy chatter filled the kitchen. Liz remembered the same thing happening in this room a long time ago when her father had been alive. Dinners together at the table came back. As did the spark that used to be in her mother's eyes. It was replaced with warmth and the remnants of grief, along with a twinge of sadness. Liz knew her mother was patiently waiting for the day she would join her husband. But right now she had a lot of living to do.

Her mother beamed while looking around the room. Another twinge of guilt struck. Liz reminded herself that she was here now. That was all that mattered. Her siblings were home. And life was coming full circle with her siblings finding the loves of their lives and becoming or starting families.

Warmth filled her, and she forgot about her problems for a little while. If she'd known home would feel this magical, she would have come here a long time ago.

No. It wouldn't have been the same. The air was lighter now that Duncan was gone. It was awful to think but true. He'd cast a heavy cloud over the family for far too long. And seeing her mother's spark return gave Liz hope for the future.

"We should probably go," she said to Dillen.

He shook his head as his lips compressed into a frown. "You belong here. I don't. You should stay while I find the bastard who killed my father."

"You're not leaving without me," she insisted.

But he got up and walked out anyway.

Liz heaved a sigh. She couldn't…*wouldn't* force Dillen to be with her no matter how much the fact that he'd just left had shattered her heart. For the first time in Liz's life, she looked around a room and felt an ache in her chest…she felt an aloneness she'd never experienced before, and she feared it had everything to do with Dillen.

DILLEN STARTED TOWARD the truck, veered right for reasons he couldn't explain and ended up in the barn. Being around animals was a helluva lot easier than people. People were complicated.

"Who's there?" Deacon asked as he came out of the office.

Dillen bit back a curse. "Sorry. I didn't realize anyone was in here."

"You're welcome to stick around," Deacon said, leaning against a post. "Just me and the animals in here most of the time."

"Congratulations, by the way," he stated. "You've worked here for as long as I can remember."

The older man cracked a smile. "You turned me down when I offered you a job back in high school."

"Couldn't stand the thought of working on Hayes property," Dillen admitted. "I'm not proud of the fact now—because I probably needed that job."

"We all do stupid things from time to time," Deacon said. His expression turned serious. "I'm sorry to hear about your pop."

The sincerity in his voice touched Dillen. "Thank you."

"He was a good man," Deacon said, crossing his legs at the ankles and looking down at his boots. "The world needs more good men like him."

"How well did you know Pop?" Dillen asked, hoping the foreman might know something about the blonde.

"Not very," Deacon admitted. "But he always had a quick smile and a wave every time we passed each other no matter what else was going on."

"I used to joke Pop had one mood," he said, smiling at the recollection.

"Your pop was always in a good mood. Didn't know a stranger and was happy to be alive. Never complained."

Didn't know a stranger. Those words resonated. It would've been easy for the blonde woman to take advantage of Pop. But what had she wanted from him?

"No, he didn't," Dillen said. "I took that for granted when I was kid. Somehow only saw his faults."

"Easy to do," Deacon said. "Plus, you shouldn't be so hard on yourself. You were just a kid thrown into a circumstance not many would handle well with your mom leaving the way she did."

Since Deacon hadn't known Pop, Dillen figured the foreman hadn't known his mother, either. But it was nice of him to offer his sympathy.

"Well, I've got work to do," Deacon said. "Stay as long as you'd like. It's always nice to have company around."

"I appreciate it," Dillen said, but he needed to circle back and apologize to Liz for snapping at her a few minutes ago. He couldn't think straight in the kitchen with all the family around. It made him want something he knew better than to expect…a family of his own.

Since he'd never wanted a wife and kids, he'd been thrown for a loop, and his anger had momentarily taken the wheel. It was the reason he'd decided to get some fresh air. Because it had also occurred to him that after Macy and Rosa being murdered, Liz might be a whole lot safer here at the ranch with full-time security while surrounded by family. He couldn't selfishly put her at risk.

Footsteps behind him caught his attention. They were light enough to be female, and the gait sounded like Liz.

"Hey," came the familiar voice from behind.

Dillen turned around and issued a sharp sigh. "I pushed you away in there because I don't know if I can keep you safe."

"I'm a grown woman, Dillen. Don't you think I deserve a say?"

He nodded. "That's the reason I'm in here and not in Pop's truck headed back home." He took a step toward her to close the gap between them. "The thing is I'd never be able to forgive myself if anything bad happened to you."

"I feel the same way about you," she said, meeting his gaze and holding on to it. "If we're together, we can watch each other's backs. If we're apart, the risk goes up. That's the way I see it."

He listened because she was right. She deserved to have a say.

"Okay," he said. "If you want to come with me, I have no plans to stop you." He didn't add the part about not being able to resist her in more ways than he cared to count. That realization was best kept to himself.

Deacon emerged from the office again. "Good to see you here, Liz."

She ran over and gave the foreman a hug. "I didn't realize how much I'd missed this place."

"Does that mean you're thinking about sticking around?" he asked.

Liz twisted her fingers together like she did when she was nervous or on the verge of making a decision. "I'm definitely planning to be more of a fixture around here. Beyond that, I haven't decided yet."

"I miss saddling up with you," Deacon said with a smile, his sun-worn skin making him all that much more real as a human.

"We will definitely ride together again soon," she said, her face bright with a smile. "I promise."

"Bring this guy around, too," Deacon said. "I'm guessing he can handle his own on a horse. We can all go out together."

As much as Dillen appreciated the invitation, he'd be shipping off soon enough to a place where he'd be riding shotgun in a Humvee instead of on the back of a horse. "I'll keep it in mind."

Liz must have read between the lines because she frowned but quickly recovered. "We should probably get going back to your dad's place."

"Drive careful," Deacon said. Then his gaze widened. "That's across the way from Rosa and Macy's place, isn't it?"

"Yes, sir," Dillen supplied.

A look of fear crossed Deacon's features. "Be careful. Both of you. You hear?"

"We do, and we will," Liz supplied before giving another brief hug. "Thanks for caring about this family over the years. I know my brothers looked up to you after our father…"

Liz tucked her chin to her chest and sniffled. She brought her hand up to discreetly wipe away rogue tears. "You know what I mean."

"I do," he said before adding, "and I will continue to do so."

This time as they left the barn, Dillen reached for Liz's hand. He had nothing more to promise her than right here, right now. Could it be enough?

Hand in hand, they walked to the truck. Marla came running out the back door holding a stack of plastic containers in her hand.

"Take these," she said, handing them over. "And come back soon. Okay?"

Her gaze bounced from Liz to Dillen and back. "I mean both of you, in case that wasn't clear."

"Yes, ma'am," Dillen said with a smile. He took the offerings and then placed them on the small bench seat in back of the truck before shutting the door.

"Good," Marla said before bringing each one into a hug. She headed back inside after excusing herself with a self-satisfied smile.

Dillen stopped himself from opening the passenger door mid-reach. "Are you one-hundred-percent certain this is what you want to do? Because you have a family who loves you in there and you don't have to go home with me. We can still work on the investigation together using our phones. You don't have to physically be with me." He turned around to face Liz.

"Are you trying to push me away again, Dillen Bullard?" she asked, balled fist on her hip.

"No," he said. "But you should think about what you're getting into with me."

"You don't think I already have?"

"I didn't say that exactly," he admitted with a smirk. She wasn't backing down, and it was just one of many qualities he loved about her. Loved?

It was too soon for the *L* word. Dillen backed off, taking a physical step to the side.

"Good," she said before opening the door and then sliding into the passenger seat before he could say another word. By the time Dillen had claimed the driver's side, she was belted in.

Being around her family, even for a little while, had showed him how good a family could be. He was beginning to rethink all his preconceived notions about what it would be like to settle down. He could see himself with Liz, surrounded by all her brothers, sister and sisters-in-law.

Liz's cell phone rang. She checked the screen. "Granny?"

She answered on the second ring. "Okay. I'll see if he's... No, he's right here." There was a pause. "I don't think so."

He glanced over and shot a quizzical look.

"She wants to speak to you," Liz said.

"You can put the call on speaker," he offered, wondering if he'd left something behind. His phone, wallet, keys were on him, so...

"Dillen?" Granny's voice sounded deceptively sweet.

"Yes, ma'am," Dillen said, a little scared of the senior citizen for reasons he didn't care to examine.

"I want you to listen real close to what I have to say," Granny said.

"Yes, ma'am." Why did he feel like he was about to be dressed down by his old drill sergeant?

"You take good care of my granddaughter. You hear?" Granny continued.

"I can take care of myself, thank you very much," Liz interjected.

"Lizzie," Granny scolded. "Was I talking to you?"

Dillen would laugh if he didn't think he would end up in the doghouse with Liz.

"No, ma'am," Liz said like a kindergartner who'd just been scolded on the playground.

Granny was a force to be reckoned with.

"Okay, then," she said. "Let me continue speaking to Dillen."

"I'm right here and can hear everything you say, Granny. So, watch it," Liz warned.

"Well, then, I stand corrected," Granny said, a playful hint to her tone. "I'd better mind my p's and q's."

"Yes, you better," Liz stated, unfazed but also kidding.

"Dillen," Granny started again.

"Yes, ma'am."

"You have to stop calling me ma'am because I keep looking over my shoulder for my mother-in-law," Granny quipped. "She was a mean old bitty."

Well, now Dillen really laughed. He couldn't help it. Granny was a cutup. "I can't imagine anyone who wouldn't love you."

"She didn't think I was good enough for her son," Granny said, muttering a curse.

"Granny!" Liz interjected. "Keep it PG-13, okay?"

"I'm too old to have my mouth washed out with soap," Granny said before issuing a loaded sigh. "But all right. I'm an old woman who doesn't have much time left on this earth, so I'll cut to the chase."

Dillen couldn't help but smile. "Go on."

"You hurt my grandbaby, and I'll have to hunt you down and—"

"Granny!" Liz shook her head but laughed.

"I got it," Dillen said. "Don't worry about me."

"Good," Granny said before making an excuse and hanging up before Liz could get on her case again.

"Gotta love Granny," Liz quipped as she tucked her cell phone inside her purse.

He wasn't so worried about hurting Liz as much as the other way around at this point. Because leaving her to go back overseas was going to kill him.

Chapter Twenty

Liz would've been mortified except it wouldn't do any good. Granny was her own phenomenon, and there was no going up against a machine like her.

"Well, that was fun," Dillen said. Thankfully, his sense of humor was intact.

"You know, as wild as this might sound, I miss that," she admitted. "All of it. Even the ridiculous things I never thought I'd miss like my brothers being overprotective."

"They seemed all right to me," he said.

"Because you haven't seen all the text messages I've received since leaving the ranch," she said before realizing how that might come across. "They're just concerned about me and wanted to—"

"Don't worry about it," he said like it was nothing. "What kind of big brothers would they be if they didn't try to protect you?"

"I mean, technically, I'm the third oldest in the whole family, but whatever," she said.

"You're so old," he quipped. "I should have realized it when you whipped out your AARP card at lunch."

"Funny guy," she said. "You do realize we're the same age."

"I was just saying how young you are," he said with a chuckle. "You have a good family, by the way." His comment came out of the blue.

"I've been wondering why we allowed one poison to destroy the whole family unit," she admitted.

"Your mother was grieving, and the rest of you were kids when your father died," he pointed out.

He was right.

"Still, why is it so easy to fixate on the one bad thing instead of staying focused on the good we do have?"

"If you figure that out, you deserve a medal," he said with half smile. "Your inheritance means you don't have to work again if you don't want to. That's definitely a good thing."

"Yep," she said. "Still doesn't change anything for me."

"I thought you might see it as a way to back off work some," he said. "You can afford to hire more folks now."

"Work has always been my escape," she said, astonishing herself with the admission. She hadn't really realized it until now. "It's more to me than a paycheck."

"That's fair."

"Building the business proved to me that I could take care of myself no matter what else was going on in life," she continued. "That has always been important to me."

"I can see why," he said. "You're amazing, Liz. You've created a successful business on your own. Few folks can say that. I imagine you'll find some charity to give a good portion of your inheritance to."

She nodded. "I plan to let the rest sit for a little while and, to be honest, forget it's even there. The last thing I want to do is focus on it."

"Sounds like a good plan," he said. The fact that he sounded impressed brought on a sense of pride. She didn't need his approval, or anyone else's for that matter, but it still felt good. In the short time they'd known each other, his opinion had come to matter more than most. Then again, in a way they'd known each other nearly two decades.

Driving back to the trailer meant going past Rosa and Macy's house. She hoped the fire marshal found evidence to prove the explosion had been a crime and not an accident. Her heart hurt at the thought of the sisters being gone. It all happened so suddenly. The fixed pupils were burned into Liz's memory. They'd been nothing but kind to her. They'd welcomed her into their home.

"Do they have any family?" she asked as they drove past.

"No children or husbands," he supplied. "The only reason I know is because Pop talked about them after they visited him. There were times when he had them stop by when we were on a call so they could say hello."

He pulled onto the parking pad behind Liz's sedan. It was already dark outside and getting late. It had been a full day. Liz's stomach picked that moment to remind her they hadn't eaten dinner yet. At least they had plenty of food now that her mother had loaded them up with meals.

There wasn't much better than home cooking. Being able to heat something up in the microwave sounded perfect at the moment.

Dillen made his way around the front of the truck to open her door. They both carried a stack of plastic containers. There was enough food here to get by on for a solid week at least. Liz had been afraid to go home for the big announcement on so many levels because she'd feared her mother was going to deliver bad news about her health. A weight was lifting from Liz's shoulders now that she knew her mother was going to be fine.

Liz was surprisingly happy to be home in Cider Creek. She'd forgotten what it was like to be around her siblings, her mother and Granny. It was good.

Stepping onto the porch, there was a large yellow envelope on the doormat with a fist-size rock sitting on top to hold it in place. The winds had died down today and the sun had shone, but the cold front lingered.

"What is this?" Dillen asked, balancing the containers with one hand and his chin while dipping down to retrieve the envelope. He tucked that underneath his arm as he fished out the key and then opened the door.

Liz followed him inside, setting her containers on the kitchen counter while he did the same. He ripped open the envelope as she stacked the meals inside the fridge.

And then he released a string of swear words that would make a sailor blush.

"What is it, Dillen?" she asked and grew even more concerned when he didn't respond.

"Teddy." Dillen bit the name out through clenched teeth. The document he'd stopped by to talk to Dillen about would complicate trying to sell the place.

"The neighbor?" Liz asked, moving beside him. It was always more difficult to think straight when she was close.

"Apparently Pop wrote a note saying he would sell water rights on this land to Teddy," Dillen supplied.

"That might make it difficult to sell," she stated what he already knew. She studied him. "Are you planning to get rid of the place?"

"I haven't gotten that far," Dillen admitted. "This was my home. It houses all my memories of Pop, which up until recently I wouldn't have thought of as a good thing. This was the only stability I had in life. The thought of letting it go feels like pulling up anchor."

"Makes sense," she said with a tone that soothed his soul. "Which is why you don't have to make a decision right now. Think about it. Let it sit for a while. See how you feel in a few weeks or a month. Unless there's a pressing need to decide, but it sounds like you have time."

Dillen understood why Teddy would want to make him aware of the agreement, but he really didn't want to deal with it right now. All he wanted to do was bring his father's ashes home.

A Post-it fell out of the envelope when Dillen turned it upside down. "What's this?"

It landed on the counter.

"Good question," she said as he turned it over to read the handwritten scribbles.

Please talk to me before selling. I'd like to make an offer. —Teddy

"I guess people have to get in quick when it comes to real estate, but this just creeps me out," Liz stated.

"He probably thinks I'll wrap everything up fast so I can head back overseas," Dillen explained.

"I mean, that is very logical," she said. "Looks like he wants to make an offer on the place before it goes on the market, though." She heaved a sigh. "I guess you are neighbors, and he might have been eyeing this place for a long time. If he and your dad already came to an agreement on water rights, it might make more sense for him to buy the property outright. That way he would have both."

"I was thinking along those same lines," Dillen admitted. "It's a practical solution." So, why did it make his chest fist?

"It might be hard to let go," Liz stated.

He felt that on more than one level, but her stomach growled again and he needed to feed her. "Let's figure out what to heat up so you can eat."

After a moment of standing there, still, she nodded. "My mother and Granny are the best cooks, and I haven't had their food in far too long."

"My mouth is already watering," he said, needing to change the subject from the heaviness of loss. Dillen could only think about Pop being gone for so long before he had to refocus or get sucked down a hole he might never be able to pull himself out of again. "What's the specialty?"

Liz opened the fridge door and started picking through the containers. She made little mewls of pleasure as she looked at each one. The sounds stirred his heart and made him want to hear those same sounds while doing other things with him besides eating.

"I can't decide," she finally said.

"What are the top two?" he asked, appreciating the break in tension.

"There's a ham-and-potato soup that's literally to die for," she said before shooting a glance in his direction that said she wished she'd used a different word. "It comes with fresh chives on top."

"Sounds good," he admitted. "And what's the other?"

"Beef and mushrooms with mashed potatoes," she said before adding, "You know what, I'm in the mood for mushrooms. How does that sound to you?"

"Like heaven," he said, pulling a pair of plates from the cupboard. He wasn't any closer to figuring out who would want to murder his father and why, but at least the sheriff was working on it now, either officially or not. Seeds of doubt had been planted after Rosa and Macy's murders.

Dillen still couldn't believe the sisters were gone. They'd been a fixture on this street for years. They hadn't had any family to speak of. It had only been the two of them after their mother had passed away and their relatives had banded against the sisters over a small inheritance. Rosa and Macy had formed a tighter bond, and they'd lived together peacefully ever since.

Their deaths had made three folks in the same neighborhood days apart from each other. How could anyone deny that the casualties were connected?

Liz heated the container while he set the table and poured water. He threw on a pot of coffee for good measure, figuring he could dig around in Pop's finances now that he had all the passwords to see if there were any red flags there. At this point, he regretted not installing a security camera at the front door. The sisters had looked out for Pop.

The microwave beeped as an incredible smell filled the kitchen. Liz spooned portions onto the plates at the table with a satisfied smile.

"I haven't had this dish is so long my mouth is practically watering at the smell," she said, inhaling a breath. She picked up a fork and dug in.

Dillen couldn't agree more. The smell was one thing—it was on a whole other level. But the taste went above and beyond. "I never knew I'd been missing out on this until now."

"This is one of my mom's specialties," Liz practically beamed. "This tastes like home."

He could think of someone who felt like home but couldn't let himself go there right now.

"I never would have moved away if anyone in this house could cook half as good as this," he said. "This is amazing."

There was something niggling at the back of Dillen's mind that he couldn't quite put his finger on. He chalked it up to the day he was having. The last few days, when he really thought about it. Not to mention the fact Pop was about to be cremated and his ashes brought home. Those events alone would throw any normal person off balance. Right?

The thing was that when he was anywhere close to Liz, the world righted itself and he felt a sense of comfort like he'd never known. Desire, too. Need. And don't get him started about how much he wanted to kiss the little spot of mashed potatoes off the corner of her mouth right now.

Being with her family had opened his eyes to what having siblings and female influences around was like. This place had been a bachelor pad, as Pop had liked to call it. There'd been no female touch since his mother had walked out. Even before, he didn't remember his mother putting any feminine touches on the place. Forget either of his parents cooking anything from scratch. It had been boxed pizzas and corn dogs in this house. If it could be heated in the microwave, it was golden around here. And now Dillen was wondering what it might have been like to grow up in a family of more than two. He couldn't begin to understand what it was like to have siblings. It might not have been awful to have a little brother or sister running around. Someone built-in to buddy around with during Pop's long hours or late nights at work.

Regret was a waste of time, so Dillen didn't go there. But he couldn't help but wonder what having a big family would have been like.

"What are you thinking about?" Liz interrupted his revelry.

"Families," he supplied.

"Mine can be a handful, but I wouldn't trade any one of them for the world," she said. "You know?"

"I wish I did," he said. "Almost all my memories are of me and Pop."

It occurred to him that his mother had at least had the courtesy to wait until Dillen had been old enough to go to school during the day before she'd disappeared. Had that been the plan all along once she'd realized married life was going to be way harder than she'd expected?

There were times when he wished he could sit her down and drill her with question, ask why she'd felt the need to walk out on him and Pop. But he wasn't into wasting his time, and she'd been clear that she wasn't coming back.

What about Liz? If he was willing to risk his heart, could he trust her to stick around?

Chapter Twenty-One

After dinner, Liz helped with dishes. She then took a shower and got ready for bed. But before getting under the covers, she joined Dillen in the office, where he sat studying the computer. "Find any unusual activity?"

He brought his hands up to rub his temples. "Nothing but a few extra ATM withdrawals," he said, leaning back.

"Date nights?" she asked.

"Could be," he said.

"We should take note of the dates and then ask around town if anyone saw him out on those evenings," she offered. It wasn't much to go on, but any shred of potential evidence was welcome at this point.

He nodded.

"I'm guessing you haven't heard from the sheriff about the red Jetta," Liz continued.

"Not a word," he said. "But investigations take time, and he has a whole lot more bureaucracy to contend with."

"True," she said on a sigh.

"I've been staring at this screen until my eyes are

burning," he stated. "I'm going to take a shower and then let all the information simmer."

"Thinking too hard on a problem usually ends in a headache for me," she said.

Dillen followed Liz into the living room area, where they parted ways. She grabbed her phone and charger, then headed to the sofa. This seemed like a good time to respond to a few work emails and texts.

Liz made it halfway through her inbox by the time Dillen returned. He took a seat next to her, so she set her phone on the side table to charge.

"Don't stop working on my account," he said, looking content to sit beside her.

"I dealt with all the emergencies first," she said. "Plus, I could use a break."

"How about a movie?" he asked.

She needed a good distraction. "Sounds like a plan to me."

"What do you like?" he asked as he picked up the remote from the coffee table.

"Could you go for a comedy?" she asked. "I've had enough action for a while."

He seemed to pick up on the reference to explosions and fire because he gave a knowing look. "Comedy it is."

Dillen found the silliest movie on the list. Liz laughed. And laughed. It felt so good to laugh. She couldn't remember the last time she'd let go and enjoyed herself. Work gave a sense of purpose and accomplishment. She wouldn't exactly call it fun.

Tomorrow would be another heavy day of digging

into everything that was happening and, hopefully, starting to find answers.

Liz wasn't sure when she fell asleep, but she woke the next morning in bed tucked underneath covers with Dillen curled up as far away from her as possible without actually falling off the bed. The second she stirred, though, he sat up.

"Hey," she said. "How did I end up here?"

"Carried you," he said, rubbing his eyes.

"What time did I crash?" she asked.

"Halfway into the movie," he said. "One minute you were laughing. The next, you were out. You fell asleep on my shoulder. I didn't want to disturb you, so I finished the movie and then picked you up. You didn't so much as blink."

"I'm not surprised," she said. "I've never slept better than when I'm with you."

She probably shouldn't have admitted that to him.

"Same here," he said so low she almost didn't hear him. It gave her a sense of satisfaction to know she had a similar effect on him. He threw the covers off and got up.

Liz could get used to this. She'd refused to live with any of her boyfriends in the past but being with Dillen twenty-four /seven was different. He felt surprisingly like she'd come home to a place she'd never known before, a place she never realized she missed until now.

She freshened up and met him in the kitchen. "I think we should do breakfast in town."

"Okay," he said.

Liz threw on jeans and pulled her hair back into a

ponytail. Going into town yesterday had been productive. They needed to ask more folks about the blonde. "Where can we stop to ask about the red Jetta?"

"Post office might be a good place to start," he said before disappearing to get dressed.

Too bad her family didn't recognize anyone with a red Jetta who was blonde and looked bigger than life. Could the blonde bit be a wig?

Why not?

It would be a great way to conceal someone's appearance.

She briefed Dillen on her thoughts on the way into town. Halfway there, a call came in from Callum.

"Were you asking about a red Jetta yesterday?" her brother asked.

"Yes, why? Have you seen one?"

"I'm at the market on Fourth, and there's one parked in the lot," Callum said. "It sticks out in a sea of trucks, especially the color."

"We're on our way," she said. "Could you do me a huge favor?"

"Anything."

"Stick around in case the driver returns to the Jetta before we make it there," she said. "If they beat us, can you sneak a picture? It can be from a distance."

"You bet," he said.

"Thank you," she said. "I'll owe you one."

"No return favor needed," he stated. "It's what we do for each other, right?"

"Right," she confirmed, realizing once again how much she'd missed her brother as she ended the call.

"So that's what it's like," Dillen said.

"What?" Liz asked.

"To have siblings."

"That's when it's good," she said with a smile. "You should see when we fight."

"Fighting is better than silence," Dillen said.

She realized more and more how lucky she'd been growing up. Duncan Hayes might have been a jerk, but the rest of her family wasn't, and everyone had suffered because of him. She could honestly say that she genuinely liked each and every one of her family members. They each seemed happy and in love.

The Hayes family was growing, a new generation emerging. One she hoped could learn lessons from the past and build a better future. One they could all be proud of. One that was good both inside than out.

They were several minutes away from the market when her phone rang again. She checked the screen before answering. "Hey, Callum."

"The driver slipped past me, but I got a picture as she was exiting the parking lot," Callum said with frustration in his voice. "It's grainy."

"I appreciate you for trying," Liz said.

"I just turned down Maple," he said. "Heading northbound."

"You're following her?"

"Yes," he confirmed.

LIZ DIDN'T BOTHER to mask her shock as she put the call on speaker. "Dillen can hear you now."

After perfunctory greetings, Callum continued.

"Thought I might be able to get an address for you," he said. "People usually head home after a grocery trip. She only had one bag, so I might be running her errands with her instead of unloading groceries."

Dillen shifted their direction so they could cut the vehicles off at the light between Fourth and Oleander Street. "We'll join you and then you can break off to get back to what you were doing."

"Sounds like a plan," Callum stated. "We are continuing northbound."

"Okay," Liz said.

Dillen sped up. "If I take Elmhurst, I should be able to catch up."

"Elmhurst is good," Callum said. "The driver is checking me out in her rearview mirror. She might have caught onto me."

"Be careful, Callum," Liz said. "Lives have been lost over this—whatever *this* is."

"Always," he reassured.

"How is the driver reacting to being concerned about you following her?" Dillen asked.

"She seems mildly concerned over my presence," he responded. "Then again, I'm trying not to read too much it. Of course, a woman would be suspicious if a vehicle followed her out of the grocery store parking lot. Let me know when you get close, and I'll back way off."

"If she isn't turning, then we should be there in a minute, give or take," Dillen said.

"We seem to be circling back to the market," Callum said. "Hold on."

Liz held her phone in a death grip.

"Okay, we're back on Fourth heading toward the market again," Callum said. "Now she's on Farm Road 62."

"That leads nowhere," Dillen observed. "You may as well go straight. There's not really anywhere else she can go, so following will give you away."

Callum issued a sharp sigh. It was obvious he didn't want to break off.

"She'll figure you out, and that will alert her to us," Dillen continued. "Trust me—I'll find her. Besides, we appreciate everything you've already done. We wouldn't be this far without you. Breaking off now helps us the most."

"Will do," Callum said, "I'll keep on straight so I can circle back around to the market."

"Thank you, Callum," Liz said before Dillen could chime in.

"I'm just glad you're home, Liz," her brother said. "I hope you'll consider sticking around, or at least visit more often."

"Actually, we can talk about this later, but I'm thinking about relocating my headquarters to the ranch," she said.

Dillen was caught off guard by the revelation. He wouldn't have guessed in a million years Liz would consider moving back to Cider Creek.

"Let me know whatever I can do to help with the transition," Callum said. "It'll be good to have the family back together."

"I'm still thinking about it, but I'll let you know

as soon as I decide," she said to her brother. "Being home has been nice, and it's because of you and the others. I didn't realize how much I missed Mom's cooking until recently."

"We've all gone our separate ways," he said. "But I'm splitting my time between Houston and Cider Creek now even though I'm at the ranch and across the street at Payton's more than not."

Dillen turned onto Farm Road 62. He didn't want to interrupt the moment happening between siblings, so he didn't say anything.

"I gotta go," Liz said. "We'll talk about this later. Okay?"

"You bet," Callum said. "Be careful out there."

"I won't let anything happen to her," Dillen said. It was a promise he intended to keep.

"I'll hold you to it," Callum said before exchanging goodbyes and ending the call.

A couple of minutes later, a red Jetta was visible up ahead. Dillen had been trained in evasive measures, but being on a straight country road with little to no hills didn't provide for a whole lot of places to hide.

There were open fields lining both sides at this point. Down the road were clusters of trees that looked to be at the entrance of someone's home.

The red Jetta hung a right and then disappeared in the thicket. Dillen turned right to follow. He slowed his speed to a near crawl, surveying all around and checking for danger.

A second too late, he looked up and spotted a dark

figure sitting on a tree branch with his back against the trunk while holding a saw. The guy made one deeper cut, and then the thick branch came crashing down on the truck's windshield, hitting hard enough to shatter the glass. Dillen jerked forward from the impact. His airbag deployed as did Liz's. And then his door opened followed by hers.

Before Dillen could get his bearings and shake off the momentary shock, a fist slammed into the left side of his jaw. His head snapped right, and then he answered with a hard left. His fist connected with what felt like a tank of a person. Big meaty hands grabbed at Dillen as he threw another punch.

Out of the corner of his eye, he saw Liz fighting back as a guy jerked her from her seat belt.

Dillen spun around the second he was free from his seat belt, drew his knees up to his chest and then unleashed hell, knocking Tank back a few steps. Dillen used the momentary advantage to pop out of the truck and dive into Tank.

The guy looked to be in his early twenties. Despite the cold, he had on a flannel shirt with cut-off sleeves. He had the face of a blond Frankenstein along with a thick neck. He'd most likely spent high school on the front line of a football field.

Dillen snapped off several punches in a row as the two tumbled to the ground. He rolled like an alligator with prey in its mouth, came up on top of Tank. Dillen squeezed his thighs, pinning Tank's arms to his sides. Tank bucked.

It wasn't enough to knock Dillen off balance.

Tank grunted, tried again. This time, Dillen had to put his hand down to keep from being bucked off.

Liz screamed. Dillen had never felt so helpless in his entire life. Tank used the distraction to buck Dillen off. The bigger guy landed a few punches in Dillen's torso and a knee in his rib cage that might have snapped a lower rib.

But glancing over at Liz to see if she was all right cost him a face punch. Tank had created enough space to wiggle an arm free without Dillen realizing.

The punch was so hard, he had to fight to stay conscious.

Chapter Twenty-Two

Liz dug her nails into her red-haired attacker's face and clawed. Her memory came back from the construction site. She'd turned from Mr. Bullard in time to see his face as he slammed a piece of Sheetrock into her head. It was the last thing she remembered before she was knocked unconscious. She brought her knee up to the sonofabitch's groin as fast and hard as she could, trying to drive her knee up to his throat.

Red doubled over, dropped to his knees and coughed.

She bolted in the opposite direction but was stopped short on her second step. Red's lanky fingers wrapped around her ankle like a vise. She stumbled forward with her other foot before face-planting onto the unforgiving dirt.

Liz sucked in a breath and let out a scream, using all her energy to kick so she could break free from the man's grip. His hand was on her like glue. There was no room to move.

She curled up and then twisted around, trying anything to break his grip. That didn't work, either.

There was no time to give up. She clawed her fingers into the back of Red's hand. He sneered at her, and the image would be burned into her memory for many years to come. His canines looked like a wolf's, and his beady eyes were intense.

Red threw his other arm up, gripping her ankle with two hands now. There was no breaking free. He was too strong.

The next thing she knew, he was dragging her toward him as he propped up on his elbows. "You just won't die."

"Nope," she bit back. One leg was free, so she rammed it toward his face. She heard a crack, and blood shot from his nose.

"You should be buried just like the old man," he said through gritted teeth.

But he didn't stop. Now he was climbing her legs like a ladder, his bony fingers digging into her thighs. He captured her free leg and forced hers together just as the sound of a vehicle turning onto the gravel drive caught her attention. Red didn't seem to notice. At this point, he was breathing so hard he was practically growling.

Blood splattered across his face, dripping in his mouth and covering his front teeth. He looked like something out of a zombie movie as he inched toward her waist.

The sound of heavy feet on gravel came next as Dillen continued to fight with the second attacker.

"Get the hell off my sister," Callum said. In the next second, Red went flying. He slammed against a tree. The skinny guy was no match for Callum. Her brother studied her for a second before his gaze bounced back and forth from her to Red. "Are you okay?"

"Go," she said, waving for Callum to make sure Red couldn't be a threat. She rolled onto her back and tried to catch her breath enough to move, turning her head toward Dillen. "It's him. These are the men who killed your father."

The second attacker was pinned underneath Dillen but still fighting with everything he had. Dillen was big. This guy was a tank.

Liz looked around for something to help as Callum literally sat on Red.

"Call 911," Callum instructed.

She gave a quick nod before running her hand on the ground, determined to find something to use as a weapon. Her fingers grazed something sharp. A rock?

She gripped the fist-size rock and managed to push to standing in between gasps for air. It felt a lot like she'd just run laps around a football field for half the morning. Her ribs ached when she took in air. Red might have cracked one or more of them.

But she couldn't care about that right now. Not while Dillen was in the fight of his life.

The bigger guy bucked, and Dillen responded with a jab to his jaw. Dillen drew back his hand and shook it. His knuckles were bloody, and she had no idea if that was his blood or the other guy's. She could only hope it belonged to the other guy.

Because nothing could happen to Dillen.

"I remember the redhead from that night," she said through labored breaths as she walked around the pair, giving a wide berth in case the bigger guy bucked loose. "He's the one who knocked me out."

While Callum continued to hold Red down, she needed to call 911, but she might be able to neutralize the threat before making the call. She couldn't risk the bigger guy getting the upper hand.

Dillen wrangled the man's arms against his body with renewed anger and then squeezed with his powerful thighs. The guy grunted and then went crazy, bucking and trying to roll. His efforts were in vain. Dillen had a strong grip on the guy. Angry words tore from Dillen's mouth as he strengthened his grip.

"You need to die just like those old women from across the street," Tank bit out.

Liz made it around to the guy's head, closed her eyes and then slammed the rock down. Warm liquid squirted.

She opened her eyes enough to see the guy blacked out. "I'll call 911."

Dillen couldn't afford to relax. Rather, he tightened his grip on the guy's torso, pinning his arms to his sides. "Good." He sounded exhausted from battling the bigger guy.

Liz ran to the vehicle on the passenger side and dug around for her cell. She located it on the floorboard and then palmed it.

"No. No. No."

"What is it?" Callum asked before Dillen had a chance to respond.

"No cell coverage out there," she said.

"I should have known," Callum stated. Red was pinned underneath her brother.

"How are you here?" she asked.

"Check your phone," he said. "I panicked when I tried to reach you and couldn't."

"No bars," she explained. It hurt every time she took in a breath. "What should we do now?"

"Find them," Callum instructed. "Take my ride. I know I could call a few minutes down the road."

Liz panicked. How could she leave them?

"We'll be all right," Dillen urged her to go.

"My vehicle is still running," Callum said. "Go."

Leaving them behind to drive down the street was the opposite of what Liz wanted to do. But there was no choice. She ran to her brother's vehicle and claimed the driver's seat. Phone in hand, she backed out of the drive and then sped down the farm road.

Every few seconds, Liz glanced down and checked her phone.

A minute passed. Then two.

And then bars.

Liz stopped in the middle of the road and called 911.

"I can't pinpoint the exact address," she began, rattling off the farm road where she was and approximately how far down the road emergency vehicles would have to go in order to find the house.

"Got it," the dispatcher said. "Wait right where you are for emergency vehicles to arrive."

Absolutely not.

Liz dropped the cell phone into the cup holder, made a U-turn and then sped back to the scene. The call dropped, but she'd done her part there.

She rummaged around in Callum's back seat.

There was rope and duct tape. She could use either or both. She grabbed supplies and then brought them first to Dillen. She helped him tie off the unconscious man while he was still out.

"Let's toss him in the back of Pop's truck," Dillen said. He took the heavy end, and she took the feet. With some effort, they hoisted the attacker up and into the bed of the vehicle.

She immediately shifted to Callum, taking supplies there. All three of them went to work on Red. He was tied up and in the truck bed in a matter of a minute.

"Help is on the way," she said.

Then Liz looked down the lane at the red Jetta parked at the small two-story farmhouse.

"How much time do we really have?" she asked, shifting her gaze to Callum and then Dillen.

"I HAVE NO plans to sit around and wait," Dillen said.

Callum's vehicle was being blocked by Dillen's and a tree trunk, so they had to hoof it. It would be quieter that way, but there was no other advantage because he could see the farmhouse windows from here. Which meant that anyone on the other side could, too.

"I have no idea what we're walking into," Dillen said. "I'd like to go ahead for recon."

"I'll come with you," Callum started, but Dillen was already shaking his head. "I don't want her anywhere near the house until I know it's clear. Plus, I'll move faster and easier on my own."

Callum clamped his lips shut like he was stopping himself from mounting an argument. Good. He wouldn't win this one. After a quick glance in Liz's direction, Callum gave a slight nod.

Dillen looked to her for confirmation. She walked straight up to him and kissed him.

"We need to talk when you get back. Okay?" she asked.

He couldn't agree more. There was a lot he wanted to say to her. This wasn't the time.

Dillen crouched low, ignoring the pain in his ribs and thighs. He could add his face to the list of things damaged. He kept as much to the tree line as possible leading up to the house, unsure of what he was about to find. This place could be any number of things. For all he knew folks could be running weapons or drugs out of here. This area was remote, and anything was possible.

A person could come charging out the front door right now with an AR15 and spray bullets across the lawn. Or there could be hostages inside. A family being held against their will. Children with guns to their heads.

His mind snapped to all possibilities. He'd seen just about everything during his military tenure. While back home, he didn't make it a habit to carry.

Rather than go to the front door, he moved to the side of the house, grateful no one had started firing from inside. He peeked in the first window. It was a bedroom. No one was inside.

Methodically, he moved around the perimeter of the house, checking each window as he went. There were more rooms with no one visible. Beds were made in the pair of bedrooms. An office was neat enough.

His concern grew about this being a family in trouble.

Dillen checked the window of the office. It was no surprise the window wasn't locked in these parts. He opened it and slipped inside the home.

On top of the desk was a stack of papers.

There were several versions of a handwritten note, not unlike the one Teddy had left in an envelope. Was someone setting up Teddy?

Dillen moved through the home without a floorboard so much as creaking underneath his shoe. He moved to the back of the house to the kitchen. Back against the wall, he surveyed the room.

A blonde female sat with her back against a cabinet and her knees pulled up to her chest. The sink was above her head.

She was crying. Her arms were extended in front of her with her wrists tied. Big tears rolled down her cheeks. He didn't recognize her, but that didn't mean anything. She could be reasonably new in town. She fit the description of the person they were looking for. And she drove the red Jetta.

But had she been doing any of this of her own free will?

Dillen moved his hand around to get her attention. Then he brought his finger up to his lips, telling her to be quiet as she looked up at him.

She nodded.

He gave a thumbs-up as he looked around, didn't see anyone else in the room. Had the person who'd done this to her fled?

She nodded again, indicating it was safe to come to her.

So, he did.

The knot tying her hands together was loose enough that he realized his mistake. Dillen stood up and took a step back. The window reflected the image of a person about to attack him from behind.

Dillen dropped down and spun with one of his legs extended. The move was effective. It swept the would-be attacker off his feet. The guy landed in a thud behind him, then immediately spun around and jumped on top of the...

"Teddy," Dillen said as the blonde scooted against the cabinet.

She folded her arms over her knees, hugging them into her chest. "It was a bad idea from the start but my uncle talked me and my boyfriend into helping him."

It dawned on Dillen what Teddy wanted had from his father. Water rights.

Sirens sounded outside in the distance.

"He owed them to me," Teddy said. "What was he doing with them anyway? I tried to pressure him to sell the property to me, and he wouldn't."

"The men outside," Dillen started, needing to know. "Did they kill my father?"

"It was supposed to look like an accident," Teddy said as the blonde cried so hard she hiccupped. "Pull yourself together, Helen."

She shook her head and cried harder. "I never should have got Jimmy and his best friend Benji involved."

"You killed my father to have access to the water on his land?" Dillen said to Teddy, almost not believing the words despite them coming out of his mouth. "You took away my only family for what…water?"

"There's been a drought," Teddy stated like it explained everything. "Small ranchers have to do whatever it takes to stay alive. We're not like that bastard Duncan Hayes, who has all the resources at his fingertips."

"You sonofabitch," Dillen said, firing off a punch that knocked Teddy unconscious. He wouldn't kill the man no matter how much he wanted to. No, Teddy was going to jail for the rest of his days, where the only water he was going to see on a daily basis was in the toilet.

"I'll talk," Helen said. "I never wanted to get involved in this in the first place. It's my fault Jimmy and Benji hooked up with my uncle. You can bet you'll have my full cooperation."

She threw her hands into the air about the same time the sheriff came through the back door along with a deputy.

It only took five minutes to update Sheriff Courtright.

"I interviewed Ms. Coker, and she said a blonde came into the government offices looking for property deeds to check property lines," Courtright said as Liz joined them.

She was a sight for sore eyes.

"I'd bet money she can identify this woman as the blonde in question," Dillen said, disgusted.

"When they couldn't take the water rights in court, they must have gotten desperate," the sheriff said.

"He did," Helen said. "Jimmy and me were going to get enough money to run away together so he could leave his wife." She stood up. "I'll tell you everything I know. I never wanted to get involved in murder."

Courtright nodded. "You'll all be heading down to the station with me and my deputy."

Liz walked straight over to Dillen and wrapped her arms around his waist. She burrowed her head into his chest, and he never wanted her to leave. She fit perfectly right there.

"I'm guess we'll get a match with footprints on the scene," Courtright said. The sheriff took their statements. "That's all I need from you right now. You're free to go. Rest assured justice will be served."

"Thank you," Dillen said to Courtright after shaking the man's hand. "Pop didn't die in vain. This bastard isn't getting away with his crimes."

"No, he isn't and neither are the others involved," Courtright said.

A wave of relief washed over Dillen. He looked at Liz, and one word came to mind...*home*.

"Callum said he could take us home since your truck needs to be towed," she said to him, looking up at him with eyes he could look into for days.

He walked her out the back door, needing to be out of the building for what he had to say. When they cleared the yard, he took a knee.

"Liz, I underestimated you from day one, even when we were kids," he started. "But I've finally figured out something about myself. I'm in love with you. Probably have been since we first met when I was too stubborn to acknowledge it."

Her face gave away nothing.

So, he had no choice but to keep going.

"I thought you were a princess, and that meant out of reach for a guy like me," he continued. "But I'm here to say that I love you with all my heart. I may not be much of a prince, and you sure as hell deserve better than anything I can give you. But if you'll have me, princess, I promise to stick by your side through thick and thin until I take my last breath."

Tears welled in her eyes, but he couldn't tell if that was a good or bad thing.

"I feel like I've known you my entire life, and in some ways, I have," he continued, figuring he needed to go for broke at this point. "It would be an incredible honor to call you my girlfriend, and someday, when and if you're ever ready, I'd like to call you my wife."

"Dillen," she started, but emotions seemed to get the best of her, so she stopped to catch her breath.

A few tears spilled out of her eyes, and he started to worry. Was she trying to find a way to let him down easy?

"In finding you again, I've finally found where I belong. You're the great love of my life. You're my place to call home. So, yes, I'll be your girlfriend because I love you. I'm in love with you. And I will love you until my heart stops beating. I would love to be your wife someday when we get settled into our new lives here in Cider Creek. You have to finish up time in the military, and I need to relocate a business. But I fully intend to make us official. And until then, I'm still calling you mine."

He picked her up off her feet as he stood up, ignoring the pain in his ribs and more body parts than he cared to count. And then he kissed the absolute love of his life, his future bride, his everything.

Real love was almost impossible to find. And he was the luckiest bastard on earth for finding it with Liz Hayes. She was kind, smart and beautiful inside and out. There would never be another person who could measure up to her.

"Sounds like a plan to me," he said, referring to her comment. "I intend to give you a ring before I head back overseas. Consider it something to remember me by."

"It will never come off my finger," she said, pressing a kiss to his lips.

"Good," he said. "And if you don't mind, I need to pit stop some place on the way home."

"I'm sure Callum won't mind," she said. "What's the errand you need to run?"

She skimmed him with her gaze, and he could see that she was confused as to what couldn't wait while they both looked like they were coming from a fight and had lost.

"The hospital left a message for me earlier," he said. "Pop is ready. And it's time to finally bring him home."

* * * * *

If you missed the previous books in USA TODAY *bestselling author Barb Han's miniseries,*
The Cowboys of Cider Creek, the following
titles are available now:

Rescued By the Rancher
Riding Shotgun
Trapped in Texas
Texas Scandal
Trouble in Texas

You'll find them wherever Harlequin Intrigue
books are sold!

#2187 COLD CASE KIDNAPPING
Hudson Sibling Solutions • by Nicole Helm
Determined to find her missing sister, Dahlia Easton hires Wyoming's respected firm Hudson Sibling Solutions—and lead investigator Grant Hudson. But when Dahlia becomes the kidnapper's next target, Grant will risk everything to protect the vulnerable librarian from a dangerous cult.

#2188 UNSOLVED BAYOU MURDER
The Swamp Slayings • by Carla Cassidy
Beau Boudreau spent fifteen years paying for a murder he didn't commit. Now a free man, he recruits his ex, attorney Peyton LaCroix, to clear his name once and for all. But as their desire resurfaces, so does the killer—who wants Peyton dead...

#2189 THE SECRET OF SHUTTER LAKE
by Amanda Stevens
Abby Dallas always believed her mother abandoned her. But when investigator Wade Easton discovers skeletal remains in a car at the bottom of Shutter Lake, she learns her mother was killed...possibly by someone she knows. And Wade's protection is her only chance at survival.

#2190 POINT OF DISAPPEARANCE
A Discovery Bay Novel • by Carol Ericson
Could a recently discovered body belong to Tate Mitchell's missing childhood friend? FBI special agent Blanca Lopez thinks so—and believes the cold case is linked to another. Accessing the forest ranger's buried memories could not only solve the mystery but bring them together.

#2191 UNDER THE COVER OF DARKNESS
West Investigations • by K.D. Richards
Attorney Brandon West's client is dead, and Detective Yara Thomas suspects foul play. Working together to solve the crime exposes them to undeniable attraction...and the attention of ruthless drug dealers who will do anything, even kill, to keep their dark secrets...

#2192 SHARP EVIDENCE
Kansas City Crime Lab • by Julie Miller
Discovering a bloody knife from two unsolved murders reunites theater professor Reese Atkinson with criminalist Jackson Dobbs. The shy boy from childhood has grown into a towering man determined to keep her safe. But will it be enough to neutralize the threat?

HARLEQUIN
PLUS

Try the best multimedia subscription service for romance readers like you!

Read, Watch and Play.

Experience the easiest way to get the romance content you crave.

Start your **FREE TRIAL** at
<u>www.harlequinplus.com/freetrial</u>.